Paris Gone Dark

BY JEROME G. SILBERT

Chapter One

Paris, France

Susan leaned back in her chair at the café Les Deux Magots on the rue Saint-Germain-des-Pres. Nothing had changed in the months she had been away except for the influx of tourists. She took in the deep red painted walls, then looked at the surrounding tables. People chatted with friends, others with husbands and wives, and some with their mistresses. How she loved this place but missed the man who first brought her. She closed her eyes for a second or two and felt his presence. Then she gazed at the empty seat across from her. Dumond. Why did he get himself killed? Fool. He violated his own rule. Dumond.

An incessant Parisian rain had brought them to Les Deux Magots. His umbrella didn't quite cover them. He'd nudged her gently and guided her into the café. The waiter welcomed Dumond by name and led him to his table. A bottle of absinthe appeared with a glass after they removed their coats. A simple nod and another glass was placed in front of her. "It will warm you," Dumond said. The bottle was soon empty.

He'd regaled her with stories of the famous and the infamous who had frequented this very place. Dumond drew himself up and pointed, "At that corner table, Hemingway ruled. Waiters noiselessly replaced bottles of Lafite-Rothchild as if they were refilling glasses of water." Then Dumond took her hand. "Over there, in the other corner, Picasso. Oh, the women…" Dumond's eyes lit up. "Picasso could do no wrong. He was an artiste." Then he'd lowered his voice and in a conspiratorial whisper, spat, "Over there, Rene Hardy held court."

"Who?"

"Dear child, you weren't here during the war. Lucky, you weren't even born."

"Which war?"

Dumond laughed. "Ignorance does have its virtue. *Mon Dieu*, it is better that way. I am speaking of World War Two. Paris was occupied by the Germans. You heard of the resistance?"

Susan nodded. "Of course. I'm not an idiot."

"Rene, to some, a hero of France, but to others a traitor. The twist and turns of his life were so…" He looked past her… "French. *Tu comprends?*"

She pointed to her empty glass. "Some more…to warm me."

Dumond motioned for the waiter and another bottle appeared.

"This Hardy played both sides, then. *Tout dangereuse, n'est-ce pas?*" she asked.

Dumond gazed intently and then slapped the table. "You are so…"

"French."

"*Oui*, very, but delightful in all of your charms. You play the game well. Earnest, but maybe not. You would have succeeded in the Resistance. The Germans would have had no chance."

She took a sip. "And if I were on both sides?"

The smile vanished from his face. "Too many good people went to their deaths because of that. *Non.* There was only one side and no other." He looked away for a moment. "It was a terrible time for all." He took her hand and held it. A smile crossed his face. "Too serious about a time in the past. Let's drink to Paris of now…"

They clinked their glasses.

Susan was so deep in thought she almost raised her drink, but caught herself. The memory did what the absinthe would have. It warmed her.

She raised her hand to catch the waiter's attention. *"Combien?"*

"Vingt euros."

The waiter handed her the bill. She glanced at the items, then dug into her purse and left the money on the table. Prices had gone up but… Paris. That is the cost. Her *au revoir* to the maître d' was said softly as she brushed against a man on her way out. It had been awhile, a lifetime really, since she had been alone in this city.

She had run away from her parents' home after they had moved to Paris from Avignon. They lived in a poor section. She was sixteen, or maybe it was fourteen when she left. There was nothing charming about Paris, then. Whatever money her parents had went to drink.

A cab pulled up to Les Deux Magots and she got in. "15 rue Jacob, Millisime Hotel," she told the driver.

"Oui, madame."

She rested in the back seat and watched the streets fly by. She thought of the time she stole away on a bus and arrived in Marseille. It was a rough city populated with coarse people and men from everywhere. She learned quickly.

The taxi hit a bump and she grabbed her coat pocket. She felt the wallet taken from the man she bumped at the café. She hoped the thickness of it was from the euros it held. *C'est la vie.*

In Marseille, a smile and nice words rarely meant the

kindness offered. She recognized the game for what it was. Women, she observed, were better at it than men. Money and beauty were both means.

"We are here," the driver interrupted.

"*Merci,*" she said. She made a show of searching her purse. "*Mon Dieu, mon portefeuille!* My wallet, it's gone. What am I to do?" She felt tears well up in her eyes.

"What happened?" the driver asked, "You lost your wallet?"

"I don't know. I had it at the café and someone bumped me. I...I don't..."

Another fare knocked on the window.

"Calm down, madame, it will be all right," he said and looked at his watch. "It's okay. I didn't drive far, and I have another..."

"*Merci,* monsieur," and she climbed out of the vehicle. The new passenger got in and the taxi took off with a screech.

She had learned the use of a wistful glance or a light touch on someone's arm. Her apprenticeship in Marseille changed her from a child to a *femme du monde*. Paris at eighteen years of age was so much more and better than when she had left it.

Chapter Two

Chicago

Billy Dee was very much asleep when, instead of making the three-point shot in his dream, there was his wife, Janine. The ball was in the air, but somehow his wife's face replaced the basket.

"Get up, Billy Dee. Get up. It's long distance. Paris."

He opened his eyes and a portable phone was thrust in his hand.

"It's Paris police," Janine said in a rough whisper.

"What? I…don't… Hello?"

"*Bonjour, Monsieur.* I'm sorry for waking you, but it is already *après midi* here."

"Après, what?"

"Afternoon, Monsieur. I am Inspector Alain Ricard of the Préfecture de Police de Paris."

"Give me that again?"

"Paris police."

"Got it. What can I do for you?"

"A few years ago, you worked on a case involving illegal weapons, *n'est-ce pas?*"

Billy Dee swallowed his questioning of *n'est-ce pas*; instead, he did a quick stare at the phone. "Weapons? Oh, the Bomb in the Palace case. The lawyer who was mixed up with the Serbian Liberation Army and sold guns to the gangs. I remember."

"We may have a lead on the supplier. Could you come to Paris?"

Billy Dee threw the bed covers away and stood. "You want me to go to Paris?"

"*Oui*. The information is too delicate to discuss over the phone."

"I…eh." He looked at his wife who was mouthing *yes* almost in a scream. "I guess so."

"We will make the arrangements for you and email the ticket," Ricard said. "Can you leave in a few days?"

"Sure." Billy Dee felt his shoulder rocked by his wife's jabbing. "Oh, Inspector, I'd like to take my wife, if that's okay."

There was a pause. "I'm afraid that will have to be, how you say, on your dime. We, like your department, only have so much to spend."

"I see."

"But of course, arrangements can be made so that the cost will be minimum."

Billy Dee hesitated, then cleared his throat. "Send me the information and I'll get back to you. Here's my email address."

"*Merci, monsieur*. You'll hear from me in a day or two. *Au revoir*."

Chapter Three

Paris

Susan made sure the taxi left before entering the hotel. She gave her name to the reception clerk as Françoise Bèlut. The clerk, a typical Parisienne, dressed in a black suit over a white silk blouse, smiled professionally as she looked over Susan's Lebanese passport and credit card.

"*C'est bon,*" the young woman said. "Charles will help you with your *bagages*." She struck a small bell on the Reception desk.

"Not necessary. My suitcase was lost on the trip."

"*Je suis vraiment désolé.*"

"*Merci*, but on the bright side, I get to go shopping."

The clerk brushed her shoulder-length chestnut brown hair from her face and politely smiled. "Yes, *c'est vrais*, and there is no better shopping than here. Have a wonderful stay, madame."

"*Merci.*" Susan swept up the welcoming information and key and went to the elevator. Her room was on the fourth floor. It was sleek with all the modern conveniences. Wi-Fi, 50" TV, and a shower and a large bathroom worthy of a high-priced spa. It even had a small balcony with a view of the tree-lined street.

She dropped her purse on the bed, then closed the drapes. She flicked on a small desk lamp and took out the stolen wallet. The driver's license said the man's name was Alexander Soreil, from Montreal. She shuddered, remembering the last man who claimed he was from that city. It had almost cost her life.

***

Chicago

"Billy Dee, I've got to go shopping if I'm going, my oh my… Paris," Janine said. "There's biscuits in the oven and your coffee is brewing. Got to get dressed and get myself in gear."

Billy Dee watched her pull a blouse and slacks off a hanger. "You got a brown print blouse and red flower slacks. That don't go, and they'll see you a mile away."

She glared at him. "Who made you fashion king? Besides, those pajamas you wear'n must have been around since Vietnam."

Billy Dee glanced at his attire. "Noth'n wrong with it. Who sees them, anyway?"

"Uh-huh. That's all I got to say."

Billy Dee stood beside the bed and watched his wife gather her clothes and leave. He took a step to follow, then stopped. "What if we don't go to Paris?" he shouted. "What if, I don't know, this Inspector so-and-so changes his mind or… Damn. Don't spend too much, Janine. It ain't a for-sure thing."

"It's sure enough for me," she said.

He heard the front door slam. "Well," he said with a sigh, "she's off to the races. Lord help."

Time to get the day going. He showered, changed, and went downstairs for breakfast. He couldn't stay mad at his wife. He was excited too. This kind of thing had never happened to him while he worked for Chicago P.D. The closest he'd come to travel was a small town near the Wisconsin border. Somehow, since being retired from the Department, he's gotten himself involved in some big cases. Of course, if it weren't for his friend Jack Sheppard, a detective with Bomb and Arson, none of this would have happened. He was the one who asked his help with the bomb in the Palace case.

He poured his coffee into a mug and took the biscuits from the oven. No one baked them the way his wife did— melt in your mouth savory with a hint of sweet. Just good eating. He paddled toward the front door in his slippers, retrieved the *Sun-Times* paper and readied himself for a relaxing breakfast. He got to thinking, after the first bite, though. Why the hell did that French inspector call him? Did he also contact Shep? Easy enough to find out. But first things first. It would be a shame to let his food grow cold.

***

"Bomb and arson, Detective Sheppard," Shep answered the call.

"Glad you're still serving and protecting. This is Billy Dee."

"I knew that before you said a word. Get up to speed. CPD has caller ID. What's up?"

"How you do'n. Haven't spoken to you in a while…just get down to business?"

"Unlike you, I'm work'n. You retired old farts are probably still in pajamas eating breakfast."

Billy Dee pushed back from his kitchen table and brushed some biscuit crumbs from his shirt. "Breakfast, hell. I've been up for hours."

"Sure, you have. How's the missus?"

"Great. She's out shopping." He paused. "You know why she's do'n that?"

"What kind of question is that? She's your wife and you all have money to burn."

"Funny. Listen, I got a call this morning from an Inspector, hold on, I wrote his name." Billy Dee quickly went to the bedroom and found the piece of paper. "You still there?" he asked, returning to the kitchen.

"Yeah, didn't go anywhere."

"Good. The guy said his name was Inspector Alain Ricard, Paris police."

"Paris as in France?"

"You're sharp this morning."

"What did he want?"

"Me to come to Paris. Said he had information regarding the source of weapons involved in the Bomb in the Palace case."

"You were asked, not me?"

"That's why I called. I take it then Inspector Ricard didn't contact you?"

"If I knew the French word for something nasty, I'd say it, but no."

Billy Dee sighed. "What can I tell you, bro, I have that s-a-v-o-i-r faire, or whatever they call it."

"Billy Dee, you are an enlightened individual. I'll let you know if my fortune changes."

***

Paris

Susan counted the cash… 500 euros. Not bad, but not as good as she had hoped. The cash would cover a day and a half at the hotel. Unfortunately for her, Monsieur Soreil had a collection of credit cards. She counted seven… American Express, Visa… Ach, a waste. Dumont taught her cash was always the prize. Everything else can be traced. However, Soreil was probably lost, destitute, with no money and no credit. There's always a game to play.

Chapter Four

Tiberias, Israel

The tall man had olive skin, his face bronzed to perfection. He looked out his front picture window at the Sea of Galilee. He didn't think of Jesus walking on its waters or any of the biblical history this two-thousand-year-old city held. No, Ahmed was concerned with one thing this morning.

The woman in the bedroom called out in Hebrew. "Daniel, come back to bed. It's too early to do anything else. Besides…"

He was about to light a cigarette, but he caught the sultriness of her voice. One more time for Allah. She was a good Jewish fuck. Her breasts were firm as well as her ass and after… maybe she had more information. Such was the life of a sworn-to-be martyr. He almost laughed. Who needs 70 virgins when there was a well-used woman, waiting.

He knew her as Shoshana. On prior occasions at other hotels, he checked her IDs, as he was sure she did his. His was Daniel ben Yamide, an inspector in Shin Bet, the Israeli internal security service. She worked in the Northern Command of the IDF, Israeli Defense Force. They met at a bar in Netanya, a resort town near the Lebanese border, months ago. It wasn't by chance, at least not on his part. Now, he was ordered to end the relationship. One more fuck, one more exhilaration, one more feeling the warmth of a satisfied woman in his arms. He'd stroke her long curly hair and gently ask about her work. Where were the troops, gun placements, and weapon depots? After the answers, as sleep covered her, she would never wake again. Those were his orders. She had no more information to give.

He put the pack of cigarettes on the table. "Yes, it is too early to do anything else," he told her, and silently asked Allah's forgiveness.

Forty-five minutes later it was over. He congratulated himself on having the sex last thirty minutes. She screamed his name, *Daniel*, and dug her fingernails into his back. When they caught their breath, she folded into his arms and in a dreamy state told him what he wanted to know. She'd linger for an hour or two before the toxicities of his penicillin-laced semen killed her. It's good to know as much about one's victim as possible, including things like allergies. At least when she went, it will have been with a smile.

He dressed and wiped down the room. Just before leaving, he looked back. She seemed so innocent and content. "*Wadaeaan 'iilaa al'abad, whashukraan jazilaa*n, Shoshana, goodbye forever, and many thanks." He opened the front door and closed it gently. He viewed the empty hallways, then put on his sunglasses. Instead of the elevator, he used the stairs, and avoided the front desk and the cameras. The side door was unlocked. He opened it slowly, checked to see if anyone was around, then stepped into the alley. A few quick strides and he was on the street blending in with everyone else.

✳✳✳

"Good work, Ahmed," his handler, Nasser, told him.

They were sitting outside of Yali's café sipping tea.

"We now have an excellent picture of where the Jews keep their weapons and will put it to good use."

"I'm glad that I could play a small part in our struggle."

Nasser, a large balding man with a two-day-old beard, smiled. "Yes, you were helpful, and I'm sure the job had its…benefits." His face reddened and his eyes grew wider. A bead of sweat formed on his forehead.

"You mean the Jew cow?"

"You can be more charitable. At least it wasn't a boy."

Ahmed lowered his glass to the saucer. He pictured Shoshana, and a smile crossed his face. "She was good… very good, but a Jewess…and a cow."

Nasser spilled tea on his shirt. He didn't bother to clean the spot. "What's a little more dirt…makes no difference. Someday, you will tell me more details about…" He fumbled for the word. "That cow." He sighed. "Another job for you."

"Now? Can't it wait until this penicillin is out of my system?"

"What does one have to do with the other? Throw away the pills, here's a passport." He slipped it under the table.

"I don't understand."

"You like to travel," Nasser said. "I'd go, but look at me. I look and smell A-r-a-b." He shrugged. "That's who I am. But you? You are anything…Palestinian, Israeli, even French."

Chapter Five

Paris

Susan didn't need the man's cash to pay for the hotel or anything else. She took the wallet for the thrill of it, as well as a test of her skills. Like a sport or a musical instrument, practice kept proficiency. She looked at her watch. At most, twenty minutes passed since she'd left the café. Perhaps Monsieur Soreil was still there. By this time, would he have noticed? She opened his wallet again and looked at his Canadian license. It described him as 5' 11", 180 lbs. His photo indicated olive skin and dark eyes. She studied the picture and thought it interesting… perhaps worth further effort. She reached for the phone in the room and dialed.

"*Bon,*" said the maître d' of the café, "can I be of service?"

"*Oui, y a-t-il un Monsieur Soreil là-bas?*"

"I don't know. We have many guests, madame."

"I understand, but it is most important that I reach him. It concerns his family."

She heard the man sigh.

"Yes, madame, I will check."

"*Merci,*" she said. The clatter of dishes and rumble of conversation came through the receiver as she waited. She took those minutes to consider the next step.

"Allo? This is Monsieur Soreil." His voice was deep and had a slight accent.

"Stay where you are, s'il vous plait," and hung up.

She left the hotel and caught another cab. "Les Deux Magots."

"Oui, madame," and the car lurched from the curb.

It took about five minutes to reach the destination. Susan paid the fare and entered the café.

"Bonjour, madame," said the maître d', "reservation?"

"*Non*, I am looking for someone."

The maître d' didn't smile. He was too much *l'homme du monde*, a man of the world, and in Paris, what could be more natural. "Of course," he said, and allowed her to search.

She didn't have to go far into the café. She spotted him sitting in a booth with a woman. He was animated. Probably retelling the phone incident that happened minutes ago. She could see only the back of the woman's head. Blonde straight hair that crashed over a black top. She strolled past his table and, for a second, made eye contact. He ended his conversation.

"*Excusez-moi*," he said, "are you looking for someone?"

His question stopped her. His accent was more definable than on the phone. It wasn't Canadian or Parisian French. "Monsieur Soreil?"

"*Oui*."

She took his wallet from her purse. "I found it down the block. Is it yours?"

He checked his coat pocket. His eyes widened, and his face colored. "I can't believe it. I—I don't know when…or how… oh, *mon Dieu*." He opened his wallet and checked its compartments. "Credit cards but the thief took the cash." He let out a breath. "At least…" he shrugged.

His companion reached across the table and put her hand on his arm. "It could be worse," she said, "*merci, merci beaucoup*."

Susan recognized the accent. It was Middle Eastern…

Tunisian or Lebanese. "My pleasure," Susan replied. "I am sorry about the money."

Monsieur Soreil waved his hand in a motion that indicated it was nothing. "At least… I don't have to go through all this trouble." He pointed to his credit cards. "That would be a nightmare."

"True," Susan said, and turned to leave.

"Wait," he said, "please, let us do something for you."

Susan felt her face flush. "I—don't know what to say. I just…"

"Please let us take you to dinner. We are staying at the Hotel de Lutetia. Do you know where it is?"

"Yes, I've heard of it."

"The bar at the hotel is excellent. Shall we say nine p.m.?," the woman asked.

"Merci. That is very nice of you."

"Our pleasure. I am Karen and this, well, you know Alex… Monsieur Soreil."

"Françoise," Susan said and extended her hand.

Chapter Six

Paris

Inspector Ricard left his office to refill his coffee cup. He could have asked Giselle, his shapely thirty-ish aide, but times, even in Paris, had changed. A man gets his own coffee. No need to give human resources more fodder. He went down the hallway to the kitchenette. In the old days, the coffee was rich and had taste. Maybe it was because a woman served it. Today, the liquid looked like coffee, but the taste... *Merde*... not good to dwell on what it was. He went back to his desk and reviewed the day's event sheets. Then he examined the pages of foreigners who registered at the various Paris hotels. Which one was a terrorist or spy hiding under a different identity? That was the game played in every country in Europe. The names were cross-checked as well as the photographs, but in the end, it was a hope and a prayer. Another case file sat on his desk... *Eduard Dumond*. He brought it toward him. The file was still not closed after two years.

The matter seemed simple. Detective Renaux's typed report said, "Dumond was lunching at the Hotel Duquesne Eiffel. He told the maître d' he was waiting for someone. He had a glass of wine. The guests gave different description of the woman, but they agreed she went to his table and shot him. No one knew where she fled."

A few days after the incident, Ricard went to see Renaux.

"A run of the mill murder, most likely a jilted lover who sought revenge," Inspector Renaux told him. He had a damn cigarette hanging from his lower lip while making the pronouncement. "What's the big deal," he asked. "This is Paris. Love ends that way... sometimes."

Ricard nodded, then asked, "What happened to Dumond's wallet and other identification? He had it at the hotel, but when he arrived at the hospital he was a nobody. No name, no address, next of kin, nothing. Only through fingerprints was he ID'd."

Renaux took the cigarette from his mouth and flicked the ashes on the carpet. "I don't get paid enough to look for conspiracies and complications. That's where you come in. I'm only a detective in Homicide. This case speaks of a love betrayal. That's all. Dumond was cheating on the shooter. He was waiting for another woman. Simple."

There was no use pointing out the holes in the detective's story. Ricard knew that Renaux would do a minimum follow-up. After that, the case would fade as others took its place. Renaux wasn't interested in Dumond's past, or the crimes he had been accused of but never convicted.

Ricard had the case transferred to him. It had been resting in his office until a few days ago when he read about the conviction of Jack Monte in Chicago. Where the story came from, he didn't know. It was left on his desk, in an envelope. The article had a picture of the defendant and a caption: *Gunrunner for the Serbian Liberation Army convicted on all counts.* The story detailed the police involved, including one Billy Dee Jackson.

He reached for his coffee, took a sip, and almost spit it out. "*Merde.* Giselle!"

A minute or two later, she knocked, then entered his office. "*Oui?*"

He looked at her, then his cup, hesitated, then sighed. "We need coffee. Let's get some."

***

Susan entered the crowded bar at the Hotel de Lutetia fifteen minutes late. She had gotten to the hotel in plenty of time but first decided to inquire at the front desk.

"*Bonsoir, monsieur,*" she said, "I am to meet a Monsieur Soreil and his friend Karen, but I forgot the room number."

She could tell the thin deskman who wore thick glasses looked at her, though he tried to do it discreetly. She had gone shopping after the café and picked out something devastating in its simplicity. A black dress that clung to her figure and showed off enough of her cleavage to attract interest, but not to the point of lewdness. It accomplished its purpose.

"*Oui, madame,*" he said haltingly. "We don't give out such information without calling." He had their signature card on the marble counter. He picked up the phone and placed his finger on the number.

"I understand, but it would ruin the surprise."

He lowered the receiver. "Surprise?"

She leaned closer to the man while eyeing the number, and whispered.

His eyes widened and he actually gulped. "Your ...honesty... it's room 507. *Bonne nuit.*"

She could feel his eyes on her as she went toward the elevators where several people waited. She glanced at her Cartier watch and as the lift arrived, moved away. Around the corner from the bank of elevators and outside the sight of the deskman, she found a door that led to the stairs. Five flights were not impossible. She pretended she was on a StairMaster and climbed. At the fifth floor, she opened the door separating the stairs from the hall a crack and peered. No one was in sight. She checked the time. It was several minutes after nine. Her hosts should be at the bar. She took her cell from her purse and dialed the room. It went unanswered. "*Bon.*" She went to 507. Caution made her knock to be sure. No answer. She dipped into her purse and took out a magnetic card. A quick swipe, and a green light appeared, allowing her to open the door. The bathroom and bedroom lights were on. She walked quickly into the bedroom closet and found a suitcase. There were no locks. She searched the case for a way to open but couldn't find one. It must be secured by a code. She went to the bureau. Men's clothes were neatly folded in the top two drawers. The remaining three were empty. She went back to the closet and busied herself examining the clothes that were hung—two pair of pants, two shirts, one woman's jacket, and one man's jacket. Nothing in the pockets. She checked for labels. None. She straightened and was about to leave when she heard a click. She froze, heard the door open, then wildly sought a place to hide. "*Merde.*"

"Night service," a female voice said.

Relief swept over Susan. "*Merci,* just on the way out," she said.

"Do you want the covers turned?" the woman asked.

"Of course," Susan answered. "Have a nice evening," she added.

"*Bonsoir, mademoiselle.*"

Susan briskly made her way out, as if the woman wasn't there.

Chapter Seven

Ben Gurion Airport, Israel

Ahmed paid the cab and in perfect Hebrew, wished the driver well. His organization was too cheap and stupid to provide appropriate transportation. Israel was a small country but the distance between Tiberias and Ben Gurion Airport was 144 km, or about 83 miles. He entered the terminal and got into the security line. Although he had done it many times, he never felt secure, especially getting past Israeli scanners. He gripped his one bag a bit tighter and shuffled forward. He had time to think.

Nasser had come to the safe house with last-minute instructions. He gave Ahmed a fistful of euros and twenty shekels (Israeli currency) for the Egged bus that would take him to the airport.

"Have a nice ride," Nasser said.

"It will take four hours. I'll miss my flight."

The fat man shrugged. "You can dream about your Jewish cow."

"My little whore is all over the news. Don't you think the police will be searching the bus and railroad stations?"

Nasser scratched his unshaven face. "There are always difficulties. Besides, the news reported she died mysteriously. The authorities haven't concluded she was murdered. If the police were looking, they'd figure the suspect would avoid such places."

"I am not so convinced."

Nasser patted Ahmed's shoulder. "Allah be with you. I can drop you at the station if you like."

"That's okay. I'll figure it out."

"Your mission is very important. These are the people you need to contact." Nasser gave him a small folder. "Watch yourself." He pointed to Ahmed's pants zipper. "That can get you into much trouble."

Ahmed grunted. "Thank you for the advice. I'll keep both myself and it under control." He flipped open the packet. There was a paper with names, pictures and last known addresses. The passport was Canadian. He looked up. "Canadian? Whose idea…"

Nasser dabbed his face with a dirty handkerchief. "I'm only the messenger. You'll be fine."

His line moved ahead. He watched a female agent check and open his fellow travelers' luggage. Damn, it had to be a woman. The person in front of him stepped forward. He heard her ask rapid questions in a no-nonsense voice and with no smile… *She's more thorough than a man.* He labored to slow his breathing. Then remembered he left the pills of penicillin in his toiletries kit.

"Next," she commanded.

He braced himself.

***

Paris

Susan walked into the tavern at the Hotel de Lutetia. This too was a place of history. James Joyce, Josephine Baker, Charles De Gaulle were just few of the famous. The crowd here didn't just come for the food and drinks. They came for the music…jazz. People filled the tables and seats by the bar. Finely dressed couples stood with their wine or liquor glasses chatting. She brushed past the throng and spotted Monsieur Soreil and his friend Karen seated at a corner table. She gave a small wave and approached.

"*Excusez-moi*. I'm so late…traffic." She shrugged and leaned slightly forward as she extended her hand.

Soreil took it. She saw him linger a second or two more than he should. Then caught Karen's momentary disapproval. As Dumond once told her, "A dress is only as good as the woman wearing it."

"Please sit. You're only fashionably late." He raised his hand to attract their waiter. "You are a drink or two behind," he said, smiling.

"Then I must catch up."

"Champagne?"

"What are we celebrating?" Susan asked.

"The rescue of my wallet."

They all laughed. Within minutes, a bottle of Dom Perignon appeared along with a silver ice bucket. The waiter had a white towel on his arm and made a show of opening the bottle. A little of the golden liquid spilled as he uncorked it. Then he filled each glass and left.

"To my good fortune," Soreil said and raised his glass. "To my friend Karen and our new friend Susan."

"Susan? Françoise."

He lowered his glass and a small smile played on the corners of his mouth. "*Non*. Your passport says Françoise, but that is not your name."

Susan put her glass down and moved her chair back to get up.

Karen reached and placed her hand over Susan's arm. "Sit."

Chapter Eight

Chicago

Janine, dressed in her robe and slippers padded into the kitchen. "I knew I'd find you here," she said to Billy Dee. "Did you leave anything for me?" There was no response. "Hello?"

Her husband lowered his *Sun-Times* newspaper. He'd been studying the schedule for the NCAA March Madness basketball games. "What did you say? I'm busy."

"I asked…never mind. Don't you think you should call that French guy? It's been two days."

Billy Dee refocused on his picks for the games.

"Put that paper down. Paris? Remember? The phone call from that French police Inspector."

"What about that?" He dropped the paper on the table next to his nearly empty coffee mug.

"Shouldn't you've have heard by now?"

"I don't know. If their department is anything like Chicago's…" He shrugged. "Besides, I can't understand why he called me and not Shep. He's the real police. You always tell me I need to stop playing at being a cop and stay retired."

"Now listen to me, Billy Dee, this ain't the time to be think'n like that. Did you see all the things I bought the other day? That wasn't to help President what's-his-face's economy. He don't need me for that. You got to get on that

phone and find out. This is an opportunity, Billy Dee…
Paris…"

He knew better than to argue. When his wife took hold
of an idea, especially if it meant travelling, he better do
something. "All right, Janine, I'll…"

"You'll what?"

He pushed back from the kitchen table. "I'll look into
it. But before I call, I'm going to see Shep." He felt his
wife's glare.

"Why's that?"

Her question disarmed him. He stood with his hands
at his sides, searching for something else to say. "Because…
That's why."

"You lose'n your mind? That make no sense."

He better think quick. That kind of attitude wasn't going
to fly with his wife. He took a few steps away from the
table. "I want to make sure it's legit before we go traipsing
off to some foreign country. Now where did I put my keys?"

Billy Dee escaped to his car. As soon as he left the driveway, he relit the cigar that waited in the ashtray. After a puff
or two, he thought about the coffee left in the pot. That
would be icing on the cake, but at least he could smoke
in peace. He glanced at the time and wondered where his
friend, Shep, would be. He doubted Shep was in the office.
This time in the morning, the man would be at breakfast.
He ran through the possible eateries his friend frequented.
One thing about Shep, he was a creature of habit. Wednes-
days was Lou Mitchell's on Jackson, or at least it had been.
His wife would urge him to call, but he wanted the element
of surprise. Besides, the worst that could happen would be
another breakfast.

He parked on Jefferson and walked the short distance.
The usual line for a table had only two people. They were
greeted by a sweet elderly woman who ruled where people

sat. Dorothy been there for as long as the joint been opened. Always greeted everyone with a smile.

"You looking for your friend?" she asked.

"Yeah. Is he here?" Surprised Dorothy remembered.

She pointed. "At his usual place toward the back. Doughnut?" She reached into her basket and handed him the small baked good.

He munched on the goodie as he went toward his friend.

Shep sat alone in a booth, the table jammed with assorted plates, coffee cup, and the ever-present newspaper. Good old Shep, an old-fashioned cop.

"Did you leave some food for others?" Billy Dee asked.

"Sit," Shep said without missing a beat. "You want part of this waffle?"

Out of habit, Billy Dee did a quick look around.

"Your old lady ain't here. Eat."

"Don't mind if I do." Billy Dee grabbed the plate and dug in.

"So what brings you to town?" Shep asked.

Billy Dee poured more syrup on his dish. "Remember that Paris call I told you about?" he said in between bites.

"Yeah, you dog. What about it?"

"I can't figure out why me?"

Chapter Nine

Paris

The band played its first number.

"Isn't jazz wonderful?" Soreil looked away from Susan and Karen. "Jazz is so much like life. We attach ourselves to a melody, but, *voila*, it disappears. Then," he sighed, "we spend our days madly trying to find it again."

Susan didn't answer, her hand still pinned by Karen's grip. Her fingers losing feeling from the pressure.

Soreil issued a running commentary on the music. "The bass plays off the horn and sets the tone. Then the horn takes command." A few measures passed. Soreil continued his comments. "Listen to the horn and the piano compete." The piano player riffed, then the horn. "They battle for control." Soreil moved his hand to the beat. "Whoa, the horn takes charge, grabs the melody, but after several bars, fades. The bass and drums step into the breach and have it out." Soreil nodded his head to the rhythm. "The drummer plays off the bass…back and forth, they go." The tension between them built. The drumsticks flew as the drummer was in a zone and the bass tried to follow. "Then suddenly the beat changes, and the horn takes over. The piece builds to a final crescendo with all members of the band joining. Magnificent."

Soreil turned from the musicians to Karen and Susan.

He motioned with his hand for Karen to let go. "Susan will stay. *N'est-ce pas?*"

"Yes," Susan nodded, rubbing her hand. *What else can I do?* She looked up after her fingers stopped tingling. "*Donc, qui êtes-vous?*"

Soreil leaned closer. "There's much we know about you, and there is some we don't. Your resumé is incomplete."

"Sorry to disappoint. I didn't know I even submitted such a thing."

Soreil went on. "You were very clever, how you got into our room. Find anything of interest? I may want to take you up on your 'surprise'." He gave Karen a glance.

Susan felt as if he'd just undressed her. "What?" Her voice meek, defeated.

"Your mistake, a small one," he demonstrated with his forefinger and thumb, "was underestimating. Let me explain." He took his wallet and held the back of it. "It has a sensor. A small GPS woven into the material. There are also several in our room. Not your fault. You couldn't know. But…" He sat back and motioned to the waiter for more Champagne.

Susan looked from him to her. Soreil ran his hand along the side of his glass, while Karen's gaze never left her. *Who are these people? Escape? How?* In the interlude, Soreil's description of the jazz piece flashed through her mind. She had to seize the melody.

The waiter returned and, in less ceremony than before, popped the cork and replenished the glasses.

"To our little mystery," Soreil said and raised his glass.

Karen joined. "You too, *notre oiseau capturé.*"

"No, no, Karen, she is not a prisoner, our captured bird. She is our guest."

Susan tried to read what silently passed between their stares. Then, raised her glass. "To the mystery." Her hand shook as she brought the flute close to her mouth. Then, as inadvertent as she could make it look, spilled the Champagne all over. The liquid ran down the table and her dress. Like the moment before the horn took over the jazz piece, there was a split second of surprise, all that was needed. Susan bolted.

Chapter Ten

Ben Gurion Airport

"Passport," the Israeli agent commanded.

Ahmed opened the book to the photo page and handed it to her.

She studied the picture and underlying information of his name and address, then passed the booklet under an infrared light.

"What was your reason for coming, Mr. Zandular?" she asked, holding the passport.

"Business."

"How long were you here?"

"Three days."

The passport covered her mouth and nose as she visually searched him. After a minute or two, she ordered him to open his suitcase. He bent over and unzipped the bag. His clothes had been folded neatly. She tossed his shirts and pants; that undid the orderliness.

"What is this?" She asked holding his dopp kit.

"It's my toiletries," he said as evenly as he could.

"Open." She handed him the black nylon bag.

He willed himself to stay calm. "No problem." He unzipped it, and they both stared at the contents... a tube of shaving cream, a razor, hairbrush, toothpaste, toothbrush, and...

"What is this?" she asked, pointing to a medicine bottle that had no label.

"I'm just getting over strep. These are the last of the pills."

"What kind of pills?"

He hesitated a moment before he leaned closer to her. "Penicillin."

Her stare went through him. He stood motionless. She waited a few seconds, then looked at the line behind him. He could feel her wanting to ask more questions. She glanced again at the growing crowd. For the first time, a small smile crossed her lips. "Strep?" She took a breath. "Okay, go have a safe flight." She waved him forward.

"Thank you." He dropped his kit in the suitcase, grabbed his bag, and without closing it hurried away from security.

He found a place to sit as soon as he got into the terminal. He did the best he could to refold his clothes, then zipped the suitcase shut. Passing through the security line had drained him. He checked his watch, then found the departure board. His flight was in an hour. Enough time for a drink. Although he believed in the Arab cause, he was not a devout Muslim. Alcohol of any kind, but particularly Scotch, was his favorite. Apparently, the Jews also imbibed as there were plenty of bars to choose from. He zeroed in on one where a pretty blonde sat. If he had to guess, she was in her late twenties or early thirties, and wore no ring. He waited a few minutes to make sure she was alone.

"Mind if I sit?" he asked, pointing to the chair next to her.

She looked up from her drink and in that brief interlude he could tell she evaluated the situation. "No, no, please," she said a few seconds later. She moved her purse.

"Thank you." He took the seat and motioned for a waitress. Before he could peruse the drink menu, the waitress hovered over him.

"Yes? What can I get you?"

He looked up. "Oh… Macallan's Twelve, neat." She wrote the order and left. He watched her leave, then turned to the blonde sitting next to him. "That security line was something else." He shook his head, reliving the trauma.

"They're thorough," she said, putting her glass down. "Makes me feel safe."

"Yes, understood, but still…"

The waitress returned and put his drink down. "That will be seventy shekels."

He did a quick calculation in his head. "Wow, an expensive drink. Twenty US bucks."

He looked at his glass. "At least it's a good pour." He gave her a credit card.

"Your passport, please," the waitress said.

"Of course."

The waitress completed the sale and left.

"You're Canadian?" the blonde asked.

Ahmed was about to take his first sip. "Yes, Toronto."

"I had you wrong."

He put the drink down. "Really. What was your guess?"

"At first, you looked…well… Middle Eastern, perhaps French…Algiers… But your accent was more…" She looked at the ceiling.

"More?"

"Certainly not American, even though you used an idiom that's very American."

"I'm fascinated." He looked over at her glass. "Another?"

Her smile lit her face. She checked her watch. "Sure. I've got at least thirty minutes."

"Where are you going, if I may ask."

"Paris, then a transfer to London."

"Vacation?"

She smiled again. "No…not exactly. More business, but I try to take in the sights. And you?"

"Paris, more business, but I, too, try to take in the sights."
They laughed.
"Michael Zandular," Ahmed said, extending his hand.
"Jodie Adams. Pleased to meet you." They shook.
The waitress returned with Jodie's drink.
"To Paris and the sights," he said, raising his glass.
They clinked.

Chapter Eleven

Chicago

Shep took another sip of coffee. He appraised the table. "You want anything else?"

"Nah, this should tide me over for an hour or so until lunch." Billy Dee laughed. "I'm getting to be more like you."

"In your dreams." Shep put down his cup. "So, you're wondering why the French called you and not me?"

"Yep. You know Janine is ready to hop on that plane, and I would too, but…my gut tell me something ain't right."

"I learned a while ago not to bet against your stomach." Shep pointed.

"Funny man."

"Well, maybe the French cop saw your name in the newspaper articles. They did address you as detective."

"Your name was there too."

"They tried you first. If you said no, heck, they'd reach out to me. As far as I know we never got a subpoena or request for our police reports. They don't know you're retired."

"You got a point. So maybe I'm fuss'n for nothing. Paris do sound nice."

"Come on back, Billy Dee, you said you're going with your wife."

"Oh yeah, who could forget."

"Call the guy. What do you have to lose?"

"I think I will," but he didn't sound confident. "Just think'n if I blow it, Janine will never forgive me." Billy Dee drank the last of his coffee. "What do I owe?"

"Come on, man. You only ate what I couldn't. You get it next time."

"Thanks. I'll let you know what happens." On his way out, Billy Dee waved goodbye to Dorothy, the maître d'. He settled in his car, took out his cigar, and thought long and hard what he would say to the Paris police.

***

Paris

Inspector Ricard tried to determine what he enjoyed more—being out of the office, or being away from his desk with Giselle, even if it was only to buy coffee. The humdrum of the day changed. No incessant phones, no papers to review, decisions to make, just an interlude… a minute or two of normalcy.

"Café Michel or the Kayser on rue Danielle Casanova?" he asked.

She made a face. "I go to Michel almost every day. It's down the street."

"Then Kayser, it's a short walk."

"Okay, Kayser it is."

Two people on a well-traveled street. He thought, other than orders, *get me this and that, we never have a conversation. What do I know about her? What would I like to know? Keep it professional, Ricard, otherwise…* They had walked a block. "What are you working on?" he asked, breaking the uneasy silence.

"Filing, keeping track of the lists of people you gave me who arrived in Paris."

"Oh." They walked on. "Anything of interest?" he asked as they neared the boulangerie.

She swept her hair from her face.

He had to focus on what she was about to say. *Idiot, how did I not notice…*

"I thought I saw something, but I'm not sure. Didn't want to say until…"

"No, no, what is it?"

"This person…woman. She flew in from Chicago a day or so after the police there convicted that Jack Monte."

"Yes, go on." He opened the door to Kayser, the smell of fresh baked goods overwhelming. "Wait… first." He pointed to the shelves of delicacies. "We'll get some goodies and coffee, then go back to business. *Oui?*"

Chapter Twelve

Ben Gurion Airport

A small portion of Zandular's second drink remained. The scotch worked its magic as the tension caused by the security line eased. His focus was Jodie. Women were both his weakness and his strength. He could charm most. Those who didn't fall under his spell weren't worth it.

A boarding announcement was broadcast on the terminal's speakers.

"Ah, my flight has been called," he said, holding his glass.

Jodie looked at him. "I heard it too. El Al 6779?"

"That's the one. No... You too?"

"Yep. I figure it's the safest. Just so you know, there's another security check at the gate."

"You're kidding."

Her face told him otherwise.

"It's not that I have anything against safety. It's so intrusive. But..." He sighed. "in these times...I guess it must be done." He finished his drink.

They got up. She swung her purse over her shoulder, then reached for her newspaper, *Haaretz*.

"You read Hebrew?"

"Quite well. I was born near Tiberius. Awful, what happened to that girl."

"Girl? What happened?" His voice sounded inquisitive but detached.

She pointed to the headline. "I knew her. In this country everyone knows everyone or someone who knows. Anyway, she died. The paper reports the authorities are still looking into it, which means something isn't right but the police won't say. I hadn't seen her since high school, but…awful."

"Sorry." They walked along the corridor to the gate. "I wouldn't have guessed you were Israeli. Jodi is not an Israeli name."

She laughed. "It's Yehudite. It translates to Judy or Jodie in English. I picked Jodie. Has a nice ring. Yes?"

"It does. And Adams?" He knew her answer but waited.

"In Hebrew it's pronounced a-d-a-m, soft 'a's, hard 'd'… meaning earth or ground."

"Good to know. Next time I meet someone by that name, I'll tell them the meaning of it. Some may not like to be thought of as dirt." He smiled.

"Yes, but others will be thankful for the nourishing and power that's also associated with the name."

"Touché."

"The accent is good. Are you one of those Canadians who speak French?"

"*J'ai parlé français presque toute ma vie.* "He went on. "My mother was from Saint-Germain-en-Laye and my father, Quebec."

"Interesting."

They neared the gate and the line stretched into the corridor.

"Let me guess," he said, "the inspection."

"Very good. *Mais viens avec moi,*" she said.

"Is there a language you don't speak?"

She smiled.

He followed her out of the line. He felt the stares of those waiting, but ignored them. *Who the hell is she?*

She flashed a badge at the agents. Whatever that was, it worked. She breezed through. "See you on the plane."

He was a few steps behind. The agent asked a few questions. His passport and ticket checked, he was waved forward.

"See, that wasn't too bad," she said after he joined her.

"Where were you before?"

"I was here all the time," she laughed, "enjoy the flight."

He left her in first class as he went to Row 20 in economy. At least he had a window seat. He settled in. He peered at the scene on the tarmac. The baggage truck approached the plane. Other vehicles moved away. Several people, perhaps mechanics or officials, were off to the left in a discussion. He chuckled. Israelis don't discuss, they argue. An older man took the seat next to him. He glanced at him, then looked toward the front of the plane to catch a glimpse of Jodi. Who was she?

Chapter Thirteen

Paris

Susan had a five-second head start to escape Monsieur Soreil and his friend Karen. Five seconds. Dumond's saying, "Surprise overcomes a month's planning," popped into her head. She bumped waiters, "*Excusez-moi*," stepped on dancing couples' toes, "*pardonnez-moi*," but didn't stop until she left the café. She slowed as she passed the hotel's front desk. The clerk who wore glasses wasn't there. She never ran, but walked in a hurry. She ignored the cab line at the front door. Too easy for Soreil to trace. She was taught well on how to vanish. Her pace slowed as she got farther from the Lutetia. Time, though, ticked. She was too easy to spot ,being alone in her black dress and heels. She went down the rue de Sèvres to rue Madame, and made sure to stay in the shadows. Her destination was the bar at the Hotel La Villa Madame. There would be a crowd this time of night. Her room at her hotel was no longer an option, at least for this night.

***

The flight from Israel to Paris was uneventful. Ahmed's seatmate was a large older man who slept most of the way.

The old man made it clear he was not a conversationalist. He only spoke a few words when the stewardess brought food and beverages. Every now and then, Ahmed could see a flash of Jodi's blonde hair in first class. Twice he woke the old man.

"Excuse me," Ahmed said, only to repeat it several times. "Bathroom." The old man grunted and shifted his legs a smidge. Ahmed teetered as he finessed his way around the old man. He maneuvered himself down the aisle toward Jodi. She was furiously typing on her computer.

"What, all work no play?" he said.

She looked up and smiled. "Have to get this done before I reach London." She went back to her computer screen and Ahmed to his seat.

After a four-and-a–half-hour flight, the plane landed at Charles De Gaulle Airport. It was night. Ahmed again squeezed by his seatmate and reached for his luggage. He could see Jodi hadn't moved.

"Enjoy London," he said.

She looked up from her computer. "What? Paris already? That's what work does." She laughed. "Do you have a card? I'm in London for two days, then I'll be here. We could have a drink."

"Yes…a card?" He tapped his pockets. "No, but I'll be staying at the… hold on." He heard a man groan behind him. "Hotel La something Madame. Crazy name for a hotel."

"I'll check it out," she said. "Paris shouldn't be all work. Enjoy." Then she repeated it in French. "*Paris ne devrait pas être tout le travail. Prendre plaisir.*"

"Sounds so much better," he smiled. "Your French accent is perfect."

He nodded and moved forward. He reminded himself of an old Arab proverb: "Be wary around your enemy once, and your friend a thousand times. A double-crossing friend knows more about what harms you." He caught a glimpse of her blonde hair as he exited the plane.

***

Paris

Susan walked down the flight of stairs that wound down to the bar. At the bottom, attached to the highly polished wood post, was a high-heel woman's shoe that guarded the entry. A few feet from there, a pianist softly played in the background, à la the movie *Casablanca.*

She found a small table with a view of the entrance. Cigarettes were still permitted and a haze of smoke added to the intimacy. An empty martini glass rested on her table. She thought about having another as she surveyed the scene. There was no hurry, though. A few of the men had worked up their courage and asked her to dance. She politely declined. Something about them didn't catch her fancy. Although by the end of the night… She chose to think about something else. She had the gnawing feeling that her afternoon encounter at Les Deux Magots with Soreil was not by chance. *Preposterous.* She drummed her fingers on the table, and momentarily closed her eyes to picture the scene. *How could Soreil have timed his entrance at that café? The place was crowded. He couldn't have seen…* She opened her eyes. A man stood by her table.

"You look deep in thought. Not something done in a place like this."

"No? Why not?" she asked. "The music is light. The crowd noise makes it easier to lose oneself."

"Do you want to be lost?"

She eyed him. He had dark features and his olive skin

was sun-kissed. His French wasn't Parisian, but south of it. "It depends on time and place," she answered.

He drew out the other chair and sat. "Another drink?"

She played with the stem of her empty glass. "Why not. Can only be lost for so long. Perhaps I am found."

***

Inspector Ricard paid for the coffees and pastries that afternoon and led Giselle to a corner table. "Much better than the station. *N'est-ce pas?*"

She nodded.

What else could she do. I am a bumbling middle-aged man whose fantasies are… He took a sip of his coffee. "Ahhh. This has taste and body worthy to be considered coffee." She hadn't touched her cup.

"You don't…"

"No… it's too hot. I have to wait until it's cool."

"I see." He bit into his croissant. The chocolate oozed out the sides. "I eat like a pig. Excuse me, but it is delicious."

She smiled. "I do that too." She held up her apple pastry and did the same.

"See?" She used a napkin to wipe her face.

"We're pigs." He took another sip of coffee and let the moment wash over him. What his eyes wanted, his head said *non*. He cleared his throat. "You said something about a woman who came from Chicago?"

She took another bite, chewed, and swallowed. "Yes, her ticket and passport had her name as Simone Dubois."

"Yes, so?"

"Well, whoever she was disappeared."

"*Que voulez-vous dire?*"

Giselle blew into her cup before she drank.

"Cool enough?"

She quickly put the mug down. "Hot"

"Have more of your pastry."

She did and tried the coffee again. "Perfect," she said.

"*Bon,* now about this Dubois…"

"What I mean is, we know she disembarked, went through customs, but we don't know where she went."

"I don't understand. She obviously must live here."

"It wasn't a French passport. She had one from Corsica. On her entrance paper she wrote 'vacationing in Paris'."

"Perhaps she staying with a friend."

Giselle shook her head and pulled out a file from her shoulderbag. She opened it to a paper-clipped page. "See. She claimed to be staying at the Hotel de France Invalides, but never checked in. At least, not under that name."

Inspector Ricard moved the file toward him. "Yes, I see," and reached for his coffee. "Ach, it's cold. I'll get a refill. You want?"

Her gaze went from her cup to him. *Mon Dieu, her look can melt stone.*

"*Merci,* but no."

"Fine, I'll just be a minute."

Inspector Ricard returned with another cup of hot coffee. He didn't mind these afternoon hours disappearing while at the café with Giselle. "So, we have a woman who flew from Chicago to Paris using a passport from Corsica under the name Simone Dubois. *Oui?*"

"Correct," Giselle answered.

"She disappeared. No trace of anyone by that name and nationality. Interesting." He recalled the news article about the conviction of Jack Monte in Chicago. "The police officer, ah, Billy Dee Jackson…" he said.

"Who?"

He took more of his coffee. "This Chicago police officer. I invited him to Paris, but haven't followed up. He was involved in that messy business of the terrorist group SLA, Serbian Liberation Army. Monte had something to do with a contact in Chicago to get weapons."

"You think it's this woman, Dubois?"

"Possible."

"What if I sent her passport picture to him?"

"Yes, that would be fine. But, maybe he could assist further by being here. He may know more of the players than we realize. A Jack Monte doesn't appear out of nowhere."

Giselle crinkled her brow. She went for her empty cup and a look of surprise swept over her.

"I'll get you more," Ricard offered.

"No…no, I…"

Ricard was out of his seat with her mug in hand. He returned in a moment. "There, a fresh one. I left room in case you wanted cream or ice."

"*Merci.* Ice?"

"To cool it off."

"Oh. I've never thought of that."

"It is what Americans call 'iced coffee'."

"Oh."

Her expression left him with an overwhelming desire to lean forward and kiss her, but…his better angels stopped him. "So, should I follow up on Monsieur Jackson?" he said instead.

She shrugged. "Why not."

Chapter Fourteen

Paris

Soreil and Karen jumped out of their chairs as Susan made her escape. Karen gave chase but was blocked by waiters and other dinner guests who unknowingly obstructed her path. She caught a glimpse of Susan near the exit, but was too far behind to stop her. Karen squeezed her way through and reached the hotel lobby. She asked the concierge if he had gotten a cab for Susan and briefly described her.

"*Non,*" he replied, then added, "A woman in a black dress did pass me. She left the hotel."

"She did?"

The man glanced at his watch. "Yes, seconds ago."

Karen strained to see through the door as she hurried outside.

A young man in a long coat with the hotel's name embroidered on the pocket directed the taxi line. He blew his whistle and waved the next cab forward as Karen approached.

"Madame?" he said, "your cab."

"No, not for me. Did you get one for a young woman? She wore a black dress?"

Another couple brushed by Karen and got in. The hotel man closed the door and gestured for the next vehicle to move forward. "Madame, as you can see, I am very busy. I may have, but…" He shrugged, then blew his whistle.

"*Merci.*" She walked away from the cab line and onto the sidewalk. The noise of passing cars hid the clip clop of heels on the pavement. The ornamental lamps that passed for streetlights gave a hazy yellow glow that made viewing difficult. She labored to see but after a few minutes gave up and retreated to the hotel and rejoined Soreil.

"Well?" he asked.

"No luck. She escaped."

The news didn't seem to upset him.

"We'll visit the hotel Susan/Francoise was staying. We'll find her…eventually."

"Shouldn't we go now?" Karen asked.

Soreil held his glass and swirled the liquid. "*Non*, no rush. Our Susan wouldn't go there at this point in the evening." He took a drink. "*Non, demain*, in the morning, we'll pay the place a visit. Makes sense?"

Karen, who was ready to march, sat back and weighed the proposal. On the surface, it had a certain logic. But… What if Susan thought the same way and decided to outsmart them? Questions…questions. Alex excelled at what he did. They made a good pair. He was right so far with Susan. He guessed she would take his wallet. It was like he had written the script and Susan dutifully played the part.

But then…there was that day when Dumond came back into their lives. They believed they knew him, too. Elegant, suave, a James Bond-like character without the Walther PP pistol, or at least they hadn't seen him with it.

"A sure thing," Dumond said. "Can't miss. There are numerous organizations hungry for weapons. I know how to get them." Dumond paused. "But transactions like these require cash…lots of it. The returns, though." He raised his face to the sky.

She and Alex had met Dumond under a different name. It was only after financing several other of his schemes, and being rewarded, did they learn his true identity. They gave him the money for this arms deal, but then Dumond disappeared. She and Alex checked the newspapers, leaned on their sources in the police departments, but nothing came of it. Vanished. They did learn, though, through underground chatter that Dumond had an accomplice. A young woman who went to Chicago. She was to obtain the weapons.

"A few euros in certain pockets lead to wealth." Another quote from Dumond. A customs official alerted her and Alex of the arrival of a Simone Dubois from Chicago. For a few more euros, the official provided them with a passport picture and the name of the hotel where Simone claimed to be staying. They rushed over and spoke with Reception.

The young man studied the photo and turned to his computer. He typed in the information. *"Non,* monsieur, we have no one by that name."

They went to several other hotels asking and showing the passport photo. They stumbled onto the Hotel Millesime. Alex presented his bogus police identification and inquired.

"Did a Simone Dubois check in while you were working? Alex asked.

The woman did a quick check on the computer. *"Non,* I am sorry."

"What about reservations for today or tomorrow?"

"I…eh, don't know."

Alex showed her the passport picture.

The young woman put on her glasses and examined the photo. *"Non,* but I am only here from five a.m. to twelve noon. This is a busy hotel, sir."

"Can you check your computer? Perhaps a reservation for this afternoon?"

She straightened her tie and looked for a colleague. "I'm not sure I can give such information."

Karen saw Alex slip the desk woman a twenty-euro note. They learned of a Françoise with a Lebanese passport. Alex had counselled to wait. He was right.

***

The bar at the Lutetia was thinning. It was getting late in the evening. Karen looked over at Alex. "Agreed, à *demain*. We will catch her tomorrow morning." She raised her hand to catch a waiter's attention.

"Yes, *mademoiselle?*"

"More Champagne."

***

The piano player at the La Villa Madame lounge announced his break.

"That is the French for you," Susan said. "If they are not on break after five minutes, they are on strike, and if not on strike, they think about striking."

"Harsh words," Ahmed said, "aren't you French?"

"Mais bien sûr." She eyed him over her glass. "And you are?"

"Je suis tellement désolé pour ça. I'm so sorry, very rude of me. Michael Zandular." He extended his hand.

She ignored it. "I didn't ask your name."

His eyes narrowed, then he recovered. "Oh, if I'm French. On my mother's side. She was born outside of Paris. My father was from Quebec."

"Sacré bleu, you are Canadian?"

"Is that a problem?"

She chugged her drink, then put down the glass. "They are trouble."

"Really—all of them?"

Her fingers played with the edge of her napkin, then she

looked straight at him. "Yes, all of them. You are staying at the hotel?"

Ahmed coughed into his hand. "I am."

"*Bon,* let's go."

Chapter Fifteen

Chicago

"Billy Dee, about time you dragged yourself home," Janine said as her husband dropped his car keys into the bowl in the front hallway. "You come back 'cause your stomach growling? Or your friend Shep had to go back to work?"

"Happy to see you too," he said and stepped into the kitchen. "Whatcha got cook'n?" He looked at the stove. "Whatever it is smells good." He rubbed his hands together.

"It ain't for eat'n now. I'm make'n a French dish. I bought this cookbook and its chicken *coke a van.*"

"It smells better than it sounds." An opened bottle of wine was near the stove. He pointed. "Isn't it a little early to be start'n on that?"

"What do you know? That's what the French use. It's in all their dishes. The chicken is cooking in it."

"Chicken must be feel'n pretty good by now."

Janine stopped him from using his fingers to taste. "Billy Dee, you just have to wait till dinner." She shooed him away from the pan, then checked the contents with a ladle. She smacked her lips. "Umm, mighty fine." Billy Dee waited for her to pass the spoon but instead she put it down and lowered the flame. "I've been wait'n all day for you," she said, "and stayed out of your way, too."

"You what? It's just afternoon and I've been gone most of the day. The only thing you've talked about… Paris, Paris, Paris."

She ignored him. "You been with Shep all this time—two great brains, never mind me. What have you geniuses come up with? Are we going, or aren't we?"

"Since you put it that way, I was think'n of calling and see what's what."

She whirled from the stove and hugged him. "I'm so happy. Billy Dee, you did good. That Shep, always knew he a decent man."

"Janine, don't get so."

She stepped back. "Whatcha mean?"

"Well…come on. You think'n we go'n to see the sights? This is a police investigation. I don't know what we're seeing. You'll be pretty much on your own."

"That a threat or a promise? I'll make do. No problem here." She held up her hands and crossed her fingers. "Now get out of the kitchen and make your call. I got this chicken to finish."

***

Paris

Ahmed led Susan into his room. "You are…" She kissed him before he finished. "A wild one," he caught his breath. "You don't waste time."

"What's the point?" She started unbuttoning his shirt. "I knew and you knew from the moment you sat down."

"Huh." He took her hands in his, then reached behind and unzipped her.

She shimmied out of the dress and let it drop to the floor.

"You are even more beautiful," he said studying her curves.

"Ssh." She put her finger to his mouth. "You already have me."

He thought of asking if she was allergic to penicillin a moment before falling into bed, but sex overcame all reservation. Besides, what were the chances?

****

London

Jodie was out of cigarettes and patience by the time the plane took off from De Gaulle Airport in the very early morning. There was one delay after another. She had contacted Israeli passport control on the flight over and asked them for information on a Michael Zandular who displayed a Canadian passport. She still hadn't received an answer by the time she landed at Heathrow. Customs was a breeze. A car waited for her from the Israeli Embassy.

"Shalom," Herschel Joseph said, "good flight?" He dumped her bag into the car's boot, then got in.

"Not bad, worked most of the way." She slammed the passenger door shut.

"Of course you did. It's what you do."

She smiled. "I stay out of trouble that way."

His eyes narrowed. "Not always."

They were on the A4 highway before she answered. "True. Do you know someone at the Canadian Embassy who can check passports?

"Out of the blue you ask. Why?"

"If I'm going to get into trouble I'd like to know who I'm in trouble with."

He merged from the A312 highway onto the M4. "Traffic not bad this morning."

"You're ignoring me."

"I'm thinking. What aren't you telling?"

"Nothing," then laughed. "You want a story?"

"We have about a half hour. Why not?"

She told him how she met this Michael Zandular at Ben Gurion. "I have a hunch, that's all. There was something about him…anyway."

They approached the Embassy at 2 Palace Green, Kensington W8. "I may have a friend," he said.

She looked over at him. "You always do."

Chapter Sixteen

Chicago

"Janine, that was the best chicken ever," Billy Dee said, wiping his face with his napkin. "Whatever this is called, the French had the right idea. Use enough wine and butter and the angels sing." He laughed.

"Glad you enjoyed it."

"Why you look'n pissed? I gave you a compliment."

She looked up from her plate. "You said nothin' about the call."

"Tomorrow. There's a seven-hour difference. First thing in the morning."

"Uh-huh." She got up to clear the table. "I'll make sure of that."

"I know you will. I'm leav'n."

"Where you go'n? Watch'n your basketball?"

"No. Basement. I want to check out a file. Don't want to come off dumb when I talk to the inspector."

His wife was nice enough to allow him a small space in the basement. His man-cave sort-of-to-speak was between stacks of boxes full of old dishes and clothes. *Things do pile up living in a place for thirty years.* Billy Dee's kingdom consisted of a desk, an old swivel chair, a file cabinet in the corner, and a 13" TV with rabbit ears resting on a rickety old stand. Every time he went down there, he'd say, "You take what you can get."

He opened the drawer and found his copy of the Jack Monte file. Shep, bless his soul, had snuck him copies of the various reports. The chill of being downstairs went through his long-sleeve shirt. *Shoulda taken a sweater. Do I go upstairs and risk interrogation or just tough it out?* He laid the papers on the desk and stared at the typed pages. The arrest reports had Shep's name on the bottom, but they had co-written it. Monte was arrested outside a storage facility. Shep and Billy Dee had arrived, heard gunshots, and seen Monte on the ground firing at a van. Monte was subdued and taken into custody. At first the prisoner zipped his mouth. Even the threat of the Feds taking the case hadn't changed his mind. Then the van was found, and a day or two later, three bodies were discovered in a house in the far southern suburbs. A murder rap was coming down. Monte decided it was time to talk. He admitted being part of the SLA… Serbian Liberation Army. There was a network of this army in the Chicago area. Two of them ended up dead in that house, along with a woman. He then claimed that the driver of the van was a female. She was the one who placed the weapons in storage. She was the killer. His only role was to get the weapons to Europe. He couldn't or wouldn't explain why he was shooting at the van at the time of his arrest. He did say he knew the driver as Susan and gave a description. He shut his mouth as to other details regarding this person except he thought she was French.

Billy Dee went to another report. Shep had subpoenaed the storage facility records. The name on the account was Dumond. *Was that her name? Susan Dumond?* He played with a pen from his desk and leaned back on his chair. He had two thoughts. This was Shep's case as much as it was his, and… Janine ain't go'n to like it.

***

The next morning, Janine clambered down the basement steps after not finding her husband in the kitchen. Normally, he'd be drinking his coffee and reading the *Sun-Times* at the table. When he wasn't there, she put on a sweater and went downstairs. She heard, then saw him on the phone. She rushed over. "Are you make'n the call?"

Billy Dee covered the receiver. "*Ssh*, I'm talk'n," and gestured her to go upstairs.

She took a few steps back, but didn't leave. He turned away to make it more difficult to hear, but she still caught most of the conversation.

"Ricard here, *bonjour.*"

"Detective Ricard?" Billy Dee asked, his voice unsure.

"*Oui. Vous estez?*"

"Eh, what? I don't speak French. This is Billy Dee Jackson from Chicago."

"*Qui?* Oh, Monsieur Jackson. I'm so glad you called."

"Really?"

"*Oui.* I was going to contact you later today. There have been some developments that need to be discussed. Your assistance would be greatly appreciated."

"I'd be glad to help." Billy Dee cleared his throat. "You know I'm retired. I…" He lowered his voice. "I worked on the case with my old partner, Jack Sheppard."

"I know…but he is still working which would mean an official request to Chicago police. We would like to keep, how you say, things under the radar, *n'est-ce pas.*"

"Ness, what?" He paused. "I get it."

Janine tugged on her husband's sleeve. "Did you ask?" her whisper more like a growl. "What's he say'n?"

"Will that be a problem?" Ricard asked.

Billy Dee jerked his arm and stepped away from his wife's grasp. "No…no…just thought I'd tell you. I want to be up front."

Janine glared at her husband. She was about to have her say, and made sure Billy Dee knew it.

"My wife and I would be happy to come."

"*Qu'est-ce que vous avez dit?* I'm afraid I did not hear correctly."

"My wife and…"

"Yes, yes, I heard."

Silence.

"Well," Ricard finally said, "as I told you before, my department can only pay for you. I hope, how you say, it's not a deal breaker."

Janine stared at her husband.

"No, no. I understand. That's fine."

"*Bon,* how soon can you come?"

"This Sunday… four days from now."

"I will make the arrangements. Look forward to meeting you."

"Likewise." Billy Dee hung up.

"Well?" Janine asked, her hands on her hips.

"We're go'n. Leav'n this Sunday."

"Sunday? No sir. Ain't travel'n on a Sunday. God's day, Billy Dee. Not going to do that."

"Since when…"

Janine would brook no argument.

Billy Dee surrendered. "No problem… Monday."

"Amen."

Chapter Seventeen

Paris

Susan woke in Zandular's bed. She couldn't tell whether it was still dark, although the clock by the bedside read 6:00 a.m. The heavy curtains blocked the morning light. A lamp they had forgotten to turn off threw a dim glow. She closed her eyes and pictured the shadows on the ceiling and the lustful sounds they'd made throughout the night.

She had chosen well. His lovemaking was full of passion, endurance, and pleasure. He rose to the occasion multiple times. In her experience, Canadians didn't have that kind of reputation. He may have had a French mother, but his actions and physique indicated a different geographical area. His skin tone was olive. She had felt his well-formed arms, legs, and taut skin. His was a body not confined to a desk.

She checked to make sure he was asleep, then tiptoed out of bed. She found his pants on the floor and checked the pockets for his wallet. Two credit cards, but no driver's license, and hundreds of euros. She then quietly searched the bureau drawers and found his passport. There was an Israeli stamp on a page. *Interesting.* She glanced at the bed. He seemed to be in a deep sleep. The poor boy did work hard. He should be out for a while. She went to the closet. No clothes were hung. His suitcase was in the corner. She pulled it out, making as little noise as possible. Eying the bed every few minutes, she unzipped the case. Clothes were neatly arranged. She dug under and felt something odd, an envelope of some sort. A sound from the bed caught her attention. His breathing was no longer deep. She pushed the suitcase into the closet, closed the door and took a step toward the bathroom.

"Where are you going?" he asked.

She shielded her breasts with her arm, pointed, then mouthed *la salle de bains.*

He didn't respond.

She let the sink water turn warm, then grabbed a small hand towel. She wet it and dabbed herself. After a few minutes, she opened the door. Zandular was standing by the bed. She took him in. His naked body taut. She could hardly believe he was ready to go again. *Mon Dieu, insatiable.*

"*Bonjour,*" he said, a small smile on his face. "You slept well?"

"*Oui,* and by your looks, sleep has given you new strength."

He looked down, laughed, then shrugged. "Why not? Is that not what a man and a woman do?" He stepped closer.

She hung back for a second or two, then let him embrace her. He did feel good. His hardness pressed against her was an invitation to an intoxicating place. But all things, even good ones had to end…sometime.

***

The morning also found Karen and Soreil in their hotel room.

"Too much Champagne," Karen moaned. She was naked in bed. She turned away from Soreil.

"*Non,* I have memory of maybe one bottle or was it two?"

"Three. My tongue is tied to the roof of my mouth.

"How many sandbags are on my head?" he asked. "Were we celebrating?"

"I don't remember." She reached back and felt his chest. She turned slightly toward him. "Did we…do anything?"

"Do? Oh, that. I wish I could say it was unforgettable, but I have no memory."

She felt herself. "I don't either." She reached for her phone.

"What are you doing?"

"Googling hangover remedies."

"Oh, please. You think there's an answer for everything on that damn thing."

She didn't reply.

"Do something about that light. It's blinding."

"Turn your head."

Instead, he grabbed the cell out of her hands. "How can you even see this print?"

"If you let me, I'll read it to you."

"It's not worth the argument. Read away." He handed her the phone, then covered his head with the pillow. "Much better," he managed to say.

"I'm going to shower."

"Go ahead, live. I'm about to die."

He waited several minutes. The sound of running water pierced his pillow barricade. Whatever time it was, it was time. He couldn't stay in bed all day. He got up slowly and walked gingerly to the bathroom. A cloud of steam accosted him upon opening the door.

"Is that you, Alex?" Karen's voice was light, as if her suffering was gone.

"Did you expect the concierge? Of course, it's me." He slid the shower curtain aside. Karen held the spray above her head. A stream of water poured from her hair to her breasts to her legs. Seeing her like that aroused him, despite the hangover.

"Not now," she said, "there is no time."

He stepped into the stall and reached for her. Instead, a spray of hot water pelted him.

"I said no. We have to get to Susan's hotel. Remember?"

His gaze met hers. He was torn between desire and the job. "Your Google said sex is an antidote. You do want me to get well?"

She pushed him away. "You never read it. Here's the spray. Use that instead."

Chapter Eighteen

Chicago

Billy Dee left the house knowing his wife was happy. It was the least he could do. After all, she had put up with him all these years. He recognized he wasn't the easiest person to be around. Being a cop's wife was harder than it looked. At least he had some control over the action. All she could do is wait and pray he'd come home in one piece.

He backed the car out of the driveway and rewarded himself by lighting up a fresh Macanudo cigar. Paris. Who would of thought? He could get some Cubans. Those cigars were legal there. A car stopped suddenly in front of him and he jammed on the brakes. *Jesus have mercy. I ain't go'n to make it to France if I don't stop dream'n.* He pushed a button on his dash and instructed the machine to call Shep. The phone rang a few times.

"Whatda you want, Billy Dee?" Shep answered.

"Nice way to say hello to a friend."

"I said hello to you yesterday. What's up?"

"I'm going."

"Yeah? Where?"

"Paris."

"Congratulations."

"You're not. I tried. That Ricard fellow would have to make an official request. You know it becomes too much bull."

"Okay? So, what do you want?"

"Don't be pissed about it. Not my fault. You think I want Janine there?"

Shep broke into laughter. "Oh boy, thanks for not inviting. Nothing against your wife, but… Good luck."

"Hey, she'll be fine."

"Uh-huh."

Billy Dee took a puff on his cigar and ignored that comment. "Listen, I went through the Monte file yesterday. There's a few loose ends, and I'd like your help."

Static came over the line. "You know I'm on the clock," Shep said.

"I know, but the damn case isn't closed."

"What do you mean? Did you forget we caught the mother?"

"How about the girl? The three bodies found burnt at that house?"

"It's the suburbs. Their problem."

"Come on Shep. You know the job ain't done."

Billy Dee waited for an answer. "Hello, you there?" A few more seconds went by. "Lunch on me. Where do you want to meet?"

"It's ten in the morning," Shep finally answered.

"It's a meal. You com'n?"

"Okay, okay. Where?"

Billy Dee checked the direction he was travelling. "Manny's on Roosevelt. See you there in a few."

"Yeah, all right. If you get there first save some corned beef for me."

"You got it."

Chapter Nineteen

London

Dovid ben Yamin, the consul general of the Israeli embassy, stood at the entrance and watched the car wind its way up the driveway and stop in front. He recognized the driver as Herschel Joseph and watched as he helped Jodie out of the car.

Joseph had Jodie's suitcase and walked past Yamin into the building. Jodie was several steps behind.

"Shalom," ben Yamin said. "To what do we owe the pleasure?"

"Always direct and to the point. Shalom. How are you, Dovid? London treating you well?"

"Very. But I wasn't told you were coming until an hour ago. I don't like being surprised."

"Isn't that the nature of our business? I won't be staying long." She saw him look away. "It's okay, Dovid. I'm not here to make your life difficult. I'll be gone before you know it."

"It's what happens after you leave that brings concern."

She shrugged and tapped his arm. *"Kol b'seder,"* and followed Joseph into the building.

Ben Yamin saw various personnel greet her with frozen smiles. Although her official title was Attaché to the Department of Cultural Development, he knew that was a cover. He tried, but could never get a straight answer as to whether she actually worked for Mossad, Israel's version of the CIA, Shin Bet, the American's FBI, or the Prime Minister. No one at "The Office," slang for the Mossad's headquarters, Shin Bet, or the P.M. would say.

"All may be in order, but how long will you be staying?" ben Yamin asked.

She looked over at Joseph, then at him. "Dovidle, how about a cup of coffee, a phone, a desk, an office? You don't expect me to work in the hall."

Dovid saw the smile on Joseph's face. Those two. Joseph was more than a driver. He was part of the Embassy's security detail. Did they have something going? Once she was his, but that was… "Okay, okay, you can have Shimon's office. It's on the third floor left of the stairwell."

"Todah, thanks. Where's the Ambassador?"

"He's…" Dovid sighed. "He'll call you later today."

"Is that diplomatic speak for he doesn't want to see me?"

"I didn't say that. The Ambassador is a busy man with a full schedule. Just because you fly into town unannounced…"

"You made your point. I'll be a good girl and wait. Shalom." She grabbed the suitcase from Joseph and took a step toward the elevator. She whispered to him as Dovid left. "Remember to check on that passport."

***

Chicago

"Seeing the joy on your face with that sandwich piled high with corned beef is worth the price," Billy Dee said.

"I happen to like it," Shep said, then glanced at what was in front of his friend. "We're at a deli, and you choose a salad? What fun you'll have in Paris."

Billy Dee plunged his fork into the lettuce. "You know,

I think that's the exact conversation we had when this whole thing about the bomb and guns started."

"That was…what…two years ago? We haven't said anything worth remembering since? Enjoy your rabbit food while I admire and enjoy each wicked bite."

"I brought the file, to refresh that vault-like memory of yours."

"Later. I'm eating."

"Seriously." Billy Dee held his fork in attack mold. "Ricard thinks that—"

"Who's Ricard again?"

"The French cop."

Shep nodded and chewed a mouthful of his sandwich.

"This Susan person may be in Paris. She could be involved with a network of arms dealers or terrorist organizations that may strike there or here."

Shep took a noisy sip of his Coke. "Hold on. You're running with this 'Susan' because the mope we arrested fingered her. Do we have anything else?"

"Yeah. The storage locker was in the name of Susan Dumond."

"Right. I remember. Go on."

"Here's the deal. The van was found a few hours after we made our arrest. The lab boys, according to the reports, found only the mope's prints in the driving area. In the back they found blood and other prints. Was there ever a match to anyone? Did they compare any of that stuff with the murder scene at the house in the burbs?"

Shep took a breather from his food. "You're a real detective. I'm going to nibble on my potato pancake, then take a few minutes to digest this. I'll make a few inquiries. We'll see where it gets us. I mean you."

"You're not getting off that easy. This lunch cost an arm and a leg. You comin' with."

"What? Where?"

"The storage company. They may have pictures or a video."

Shep looked at his watch then at his plate. "There ain't no free lunch in this world. I should have known."

Chapter Twenty

Paris

It was not unusual for Inspector Ricard to work late after his shift was done. Ever since his wife, Madeline, had passed two years ago, he had no reason to go home. But then again, he did not always accomplished much. It was a way to put off eating dinner alone as much as anything else. The bright spot this evening was when Giselle knocked on his door and told him she was leaving for the day. Did he imagine an added smile? Was there something in her voice that invited more than "Have a good night. See you in the morning"? His teenage angst reared its ugly head even though he was long past that stage. He was too old for that and too young not to notice…her shape, or the seductiveness of her voice. He closed his eyes for a moment and pictured the way she played with her hair. *Merde.* What his body wanted conflicted with what his head knew. *Trop c'est trop.* He got up and walked around his desk. Enough is enough. His phone rang. At first, he didn't understand the caller, his English not as fluent as he'd like. It took several seconds until he recognized the voice as being Monsieur Jackson from Chicago. The conversation happened quickly, his mind still in a fog. At the end of it, he committed to paying for Jackson's trip, even though he'd never asked his higher-ups. It would have to come out of his personal office budget. *Merde.* He sat down again and stared into his office space. Should he phone Giselle and tell her what just occurred? He rapped his fingers on a note pad. *Non, that would be stupid. She is not of equal rank. But, it would be an excuse to call.* He wiped his face with his hand. This was becoming exhausting. He was never this…this whatever this was when he'd met his wife, Madeline. He took aim and conquered. *What has become of him?* He looked over at the Dumond file that rested on his desk. It was a constant reminder of his failure to concentrate. *"Demain,* always *demain."* He stood up, grabbed his coat, and left.

***

Susan took in Zandular's unwashed smell. Far from being unpleasant, it was a reminder of last night's exploits. The feel of his shoulders and the subtle ripple of his muscles beckoned. She felt his hand slide down her back. In seconds she knew what he ignited would be too late to stop. Her cough broke the trance.

"Are you okay?" he asked.

She put her hand up to her mouth. "Yes, yes, I'm fine."

He reached for her, but she stepped back.

"Non, it's been lovely, but we… I must get on with my life. Everything has an end."

"Pourquois?"

She smiled despite herself. "You look like a little boy who cannot have a birthday party. Because this is how life works."

"Children always ask why. Usually adults don't give satisfying answers. That's why they repeat the question. I will not force myself on you, but at least let's have breakfast."

She lingered over him while fighting her desire, then weakly pointed toward the bathroom. "I'll shower, then we'll see."

"It's big enough for two."

***

The breakfast place at the hotel La Villa Madame was light and airy. The maître d' escorted them to a table for two that had a view of the hotel's garden. Of course, the setting included one red rose. A menu was given to each.

"I'm so hungry I can eat everything on this," Zandular said.

"I understand why," Susan said. "I am too."

"We were teenagers. Better than teenagers."

"Knowledge coupled with youthful strength, a dangerous combination."

The waitress came over and poured coffee for them.

Susan took a sip, then set the cup down. "Well, Mr. Zandular…"

"Michael. I think we can be on first name basis after our night together." He was about to take his coffee but stopped. "I am embarrassed. I…I don't know your name. Did you say and I forgot?" He looked upset.

"I don't think we got that far."

They burst out laughing.

He shook his head. "It's the way of the world. We can be so intimate and at the same time so distant. Why don't we start at the beginning? I am Michael Zandular, and you?"

Susan let the question dangle. *Names. Today I am Susan and yesterday Françoise or Simone. Names. Does it matter what we are called?*

"Hello? You seemed to have left. All I asked was your name."

"Yes, I know. It's Susan," she said after a long pause.

"You sure?"

Her gaze went through him. "Are you?"

***

Soreil experienced something miracle-like in the shower. The hot water spray washed away his pounding headache. He actually felt refreshed. His singing burst through the walls of the bathroom.

***

"Are you all right?" Karen yelled. The clamor continued, which made her stop putting on her eyeshadow. She stepped toward the bathroom.

"Alex?" She tried the door but it was locked. She heard a series of grunts and high-pitched sounds, like a dog howling at the moon. She knocked, then pounded. The noise stopped as well as the sound of running water. The door opened and a cloud of steam enveloped her. Soreil stood naked with water dripping off him.

"What? I heard this terrible battering. Something wrong?"

She looked him over. Perhaps familiarity had chiseled away desire. Or, like merchandising, the item had to be presented in a certain way. Seeing his body *au naturel* did nothing for her. Besides, his standing there was his way of taunting. "No, nothing is wrong. It was the noise coming from there," she pointed, "I thought…"

"My singing alarmed you? My apology. You were absolutely right, though. That shower cured me. I'll be out of here in no time. Let's get a bite before we go."

That boyish smile of his swept over his face. It still charmed her. "Okay, but… do we have the time? It's after nine."

"If Susan, Françoise, or whatever name she's using had a night like ours, she would not be an early riser."

The "if" part of his statement stuck. "Alex, we're out a lot of money. Why take the chance? We can always eat later."

Alex wrapped himself in a towel and began to shave. The

white lather covered his face. "Don't be so edgy…ach." He cut himself. He tore a piece of Kleenex and placed it on the wound. "See what you made me do. Be patient. We'll find her and get the information. A couple of croissants and coffee won't make a difference."

She dropped the argument for the moment and went back to putting the finishing touches on her makeup. The face that stared at her in the mirror was not that of a twenty-five-year-old anymore. It wasn't obvious, but she knew. Faint lines popped up around the eyes. Her skin tone was not as fresh. She still commanded attention, but ten years with Alex had taken a toll. It had been a whirlwind. She had tasted a world she would never have known. Fabulous places, hotel suites with their own swimming pool, nights rubbing elbows and everything else with the rich and nearly rich. It was a game full of adventure. They had run from cops, and sometimes worse people than police. It was an underworld acted out in broad daylight by people one rarely suspected. Hers was a life far from the little village in Tunisia. Her parents would never believe it, if they'd ever wondered what had become of their daughter.

Soreil dressed while Karen searched for her cashmere wool sweater. "Did you find it?" he asked.

"If I did, would I still be looking? You think that little bitch stole it while she snooped through our things early last evening?"

He put on his blazer and wrapped a scarf around his throat. Then went to the safe and removed a pistol. "The purse she carried was too small to hold something like that."

"I suppose. Ach, found it."

"Where?"

"On the floor in the corner."

"Good, let's go."

They took the elevator to the main floor.

"I'm going to extend our stay for a day," Soreil said. "I'll meet you."

He approached the guest service area. A beautiful young woman asked if she could be of assistance. At other times, Soreil would have made a remark, but he kept those thoughts to himself. He waited patiently as he made his request and she checked the computer.

"*Oui,* we are happy to extend your stay," she said.

"*Merci.*"

He was about to walk away when she said, "Just a moment. A letter came for you."

"Oh?" He tried to hide his surprise. "When?"

"I don't know, but I'll get it for you."

She left her post and disappeared into an office. She reappeared minutes later.

"Here you are. Enjoy your morning."

"Thank you again." He walked away holding a small envelope. There was no stamp, and no return address.

Chapter Twenty-One

Chicago

Billy Dee recalled the storage company's office address was near Pulaski between Addison and Irving Park Road.

"How do you remember that?" Shep asked. "It's been, what, two years since the last time we were there. Noth'n going on in your life?"

Billy Dee smiled. "Well, let's see. You were shot a year ago, and we busted up that gang that were setting all those fires on the South Side."

Shep reached for a cigarette from his front pocket. "Don't remind me. Since then my arm can forecast rain and snow."

Billy Dee looked over. "Don't you go light'n that thing. I hate cigarette smoke."

"Jesus, Billy Dee, I can hardly breathe in this car with that cigar in the ashtray."

"My car, my rules. You know how that goes."

"Okay, okay. Next time I drive." He put the cigarette back in the pack. "Hey, what was the name of the broad that we talked to? She was such a bitch."

"Come on, Shep, your brain ain't dead. She should have made a lasting impression. You came close to locking her up."

Shep glanced out the passenger window. "That don't mean a thing. What's the name? Was it in the file?"

Billy Dee took delight in his partner's discomfort. "I'll give you a hint."

No response.

"Really, I'm a fair guy. I understand your head is clogged by all that smoke you inhale. It messes with the thinking."

"Noth'n wrong with my thinking. Margie Farwell. There."

"Who?"

"The name of the bitch."

"Close, but as they say, no cigar."

"Don't want one, anyway. She probably doesn't work there anymore."

"Stockton, Marjorie Stockton. That's her name."

Shep gave his *I don't give a damn* look. "Just be glad I let you talk me into this. It's a favor."

"Got it."

Billy Dee saw the sign for the company half a block away. "Look at that, a space right in front." He parked the car and was about to exit. "Ready?"

Shep opened his side then took out a cigarette. "Don't say a word. Let's go."

They walked to the entrance and Shep opened the door.

"Can I help you?" asked a man in an open-collar shirt.

Shep whispered to Billy Dee. "Told you, she's gone."

"Great. You've got a fresh start. Get the ball rolling."

"Me?"

"Jesus, you're the dick."

Shep put his cigarette out, then flashed his badge. "I'm Detective Sheppard and that's Detective Jackson. About two years ago around Thanksgiving a woman rented a locker from you."

"Two years ago!" The open-collar clerk said. "That's a long time."

"We have the name and the locker—Susan Dumond. She rented locker number…" He turned to Billy Dee. "What's the number?"

Billy Dee's mouth dropped. "Off the top of my head… I…I…don't remember. It's in the file. Did you bring it?"

"No."

They looked at each other.

"…must be in the car. I'll get it." Billy Dee left and in a minute or two returned. He unwound the string around the flap and delved into the papers. "Got to be in here, somewhere," he said under his breath. "Hold this," and handed the reports to Shep while he retrieved his glasses from his pocket.

"What do you want anyway?" the clerk asked.

"The video and any other pictures you have of this person."

Billy Dee was still searching.

"Oh, we wouldn't have them. Videos are kept for thirty days, then we reuse them. Sort of like what you fellas do. Thirty days—that's all."

Billy Dee looked up. "What about a photo when she opened her account?"

"If you didn't get it back then…" he shrugged, "I doubt it."

"Could you look?"

The clerk's face turned red. He cleared his throat a few times and looked at one detective then the other. "I'm… sort of new…on the job. The woman who used to do this, well…anyway, I'm not sure…the protocol…you know…" He gulped.

"We'll make it easy," Billy Dee said. "First see if you have it."

"I…I Jesus…can I give that kind of information?"

Billy Dee stepped closer and in his most fatherly tone said, "Sure you can, son. We're the police. Here to serve and protect, and you'd be helping us a great deal in this murder investigation."

"Murder! Oh, my Lord. What to do?" The clerk rubbed

his hands. "I 'm pretty sure it's against the rules." He stared into Billy Dee's face. "Will I really be helping?"

"Yes, you will, son. A great deal."

"All right, I'll check. A murder investigation, golly. I need the name, locker number, and date."

Billy Dee gave the name again. Shep took the file from him. He flipped a few pages. "Here it is…Two Four Seven Five D and the date."

The clerk attacked his computer. He typed, pounded the keys, then shifted to another screen.

"Is he putting in the nuclear codes?" Shep asked quietly.

Billy Dee gave his partner a sharp look to be quiet.

The clerk stared at both screens then moved his mouse. "Ah…" he said, then seconds ticked by. He got up went to another room. When he returned he slapped a manila file on the counter. A photo was paperclipped to the front.

"What…what's going on?" Billy Dee tried to peer over and grab a look.

"I got the picture," the clerk pointed to his screen. "Can't print it."

"Excuse me," Billy Dee said. "What do you mean?"

"No way to do it." The clerk dabbed his face with his hand. "I don't have the password."

"Let me see," Shep moved toward the clerk's computer."

"I can't let you behind the counter. I'm sure of that."

Billy Dee could feel the tension rise in his partner. "Okay, how about if I give you my phone and you take a picture. That shouldn't upset no one." He reached into his pocket and held his cell.

The clerk glanced at the screen, the keyboard, and back to the screen, then took the phone. He pointed the camera feature one way, then another, paused. "Try'n to get it right," he said. He made a few more adjustments before he snapped a few photos, then handed the device back.

"Thanks, you've been a great help," Billy Dee said.

"Aren't you going to look?" Shep asked.

"It's all good," and he lightly pulled Shep's sleeve to follow him out the door.

Chapter Twenty-Two

Paris

Zandular felt a slight tremor go through him. *Is this woman, Susan, questioning my real identity? What tigress did I bring to bed last night?* He kept his smile plastered on his face and raised his glass. "To whatever name you desire. I never considered your point. And if not to your name, then to a wonderful evening and a perfect morning."

A smile tugged at the corners of her mouth. "Yes, I agree."

They clinked their glasses. She took a sip, then put the flute down. "Do you travel a lot?"

"Oh here and there. Paris, London, Rome… the usual grand tour. Why do you ask?"

"Curious. Is that for business?"

He took another gulp of his drink. "Sometimes, and sometimes for pleasure."

Her face broke into a wide smile. "Last night would certainly fall into that category. Does fortune smile on you often?"

His gaze went from her to the leather-bound menu that lay next to his plate. He looked at her. Even in the morning she was beautiful. "Not as lucky as last night."

"I think you're blushing," she said.

"Must be the Champagne. Why don't we eat?"

They opened the menu. His gaze darted from the items

on the page back to her. There was something about her face that tickled his memory. He had the feeling he had seen her before. But where?

"Something wrong?" she asked. "We don't have to eat here if nothing appeals to you. Matter of fact, it's probably just as well."

"No, no nothing like that. Please. I definitely need food. There are so many choices."

She looked down at her menu. "How about cinnamon sugar French toast?"

He quickly agreed.

"Do you travel?" he asked.

"Don't we all."

"Where have you been?" He kept his voice friendly, as if asking about the weather.

She took another sip of her Champagne, then leaned closer to him. "I've seen a little of the world, but the one place I haven't is the Middle East. Always seemed too dangerous…with all the wars and strife. But I'd like to go. See the pyramids, then to Israel. I could get into all the biblical, historical stuff. Have you ever been?"

"Israel?" He played for time. *Does she know? Or is it an innocent question to make conversation?* "We should go one day," he finally answered. "It's a fantastical country. The people are young and vibrant."

"You mean the women."

"Them too."

She laughed. "So, you've been there. Business?"

The waitress came and took their order.

"Sometimes, it was business," Zandular said, "and other…"

The food came. They both wolfed down their meal. "I was hungrier than I thought," she said.

"Sex works up an appetite. Don't you think?"

"It is exercise, but you don't count your steps."

He looked up from his clean plate. "I like that." He paused. "Unless there's a chase."

She smiled. "You have something in mind?"

"*Non,* only a reflection."

She looked at her watch. "This has been lovely, but…"

"You need to go," he said.

"*Oui.*"

"Appointments to keep?"

She eyed him curiously. Did he think she was some kind of prostitute? "Monsieur Zandular…"

"Michael, remember?"

"Okay, Michael. My work is not what you may think or want to believe. I do not jump into bed for money. I have a life and now…"

"Please believe me, I did not think…no of course not. I understand about, loneliness, and opportunity."

"Yes, and all that. But life knocks on the door and I must move on." She placed her napkin on the table and was about to rise.

"What about that trip you wanted to take? Israel? I, or, we could go there. I know the country."

She sat. "Tell me more."

"I will, but I must go to my room. I forgot something. Will you stay? Or, you can come."

Is this a come-on? A lure to get me back into bed? She searched his face but discerned no danger lingering behind his eyes. She already knew he'd been to Israel, having snooped and found his passport. Could that be what he wanted to show? She made a display of looking at her watch. "Okay, I have a few minutes. I'll wait."

He walked with a steady gait. He knew he'd seen Susan's face before. He didn't want to rush. How lucky, if she was one of the arms dealers he was sent to find. Allah was too kind to make it this easy. The elevator came as soon as he touched the button. Within seconds he arrived at his floor. The hallway was empty except for a cleaning crew at the other end. He slid his key card into the slot and waited for the light to turn green. As soon as it did, he heard a click. He turned the door handle and pushed.

***

London

The Embassy's quarters were luxurious. It was one of the better residences to stay in. That being said, London, England was not the safest of places. In the 90s, the Israeli Ambassador was assassinated. Ten years later, a terrorist drove a car onto the grounds and blew itself up. Adjustments were made. Security tightened, cameras seen and unseen. But, no matter what, hate finds a way to destroy.

Jodie looked out her window. The manicured grounds surrounded the house. Trees were strategically placed. The placid grounds a paradise of greenery, if this were spring. She checked her watch and wondered if the Ambassador was really busy. Dovid ben Yamin ran the day-to-day operation of the Embassy. He was always prickly when it came to protecting his turf. He hovered over minutiae down to an errant paperclip. Her unexpected visit must have turned him upside down. She chuckled. *Dovid, we were good while it lasted, but overbearingness has a price.* Down to business. She picked up the phone and dialed.

"Shalom, Moshe Vergon, please," she said in rapid Hebrew.

"Just a moment," the attaché answered. "Who is calling?"

"You don't recognize me? Shame. I haven't been gone that long."

She heard muffled sounds as she was sure the person covered the receiver. More clicks, then clack.

"Hello? Yehudite, nice to hear your voice."

"Yours as well. I need to speak with you sooner rather than later."

"You're in the building? Aren't you?"

"Yes, I'm staying a few days."

"Good. How about now? I have a little time before the next appointment. You do remember the way?"

"I'll be there in five minutes."

"Shalom."

***

The ambassador's office was a suite located on the top floor of the building. There was the receiving area, with huge photos of modern Israel on the wall. A hallway some 200 feet long filled with portraits of the founders of the State. At the end of the corridor were two massive doors with the symbol of Israel, a menorah with an olive branch on either side, emblazoned on each panel. Inside, there were floor to ceiling windows, a fireplace in the corner, and Persian rugs on the hardwood floors. The cherrywood desk commanded the corner of the room flanked by the flags of Israel and Great Britain. In front were deep leather uphol-stered chairs. Another passageway led to a more informal, smaller room also with a fireplace, a couch, and several wing chairs.

"Hard to believe, I live in this opulence," the Ambassador said, circling his arm in the air. "For a little country built out of sand dunes and history, we have come a long way. Can I get you something, Yehudite?"

Even though the ambassador spoke a perfect Hebrew, his Australian accent seeped through.

"Not necessary," then, after a moment's hesitation, "a coffee. I asked Dovid, but in the confusion of my surprise visit, he must have forgotten." She knew she shouldn't have said it, but couldn't help herself.

"You know Dovid better than me. He doesn't like what he can't control."

She hid her smile. "I know, but...*lo hashuv.*" She shrugged.

The ambassador pushed a button, and a gentle knock on the door followed. A very British looking man, mustached, and dressed in an open collar Israeli army shirt and black pants entered. He took the order and shortly returned with two cups and a serving carafe. The ambassador thanked him and waited his leave.

"So, Yehudite, to what do I owe this pleasure?"

"I have a letter from the Prime Minister. He wanted it hand delivered."

The ambassador grunted. "He doesn't trust our cables? He is a strange man, our Prime Minister. I should be more diplomatic, but I trust I'm with a friend."

Yehudite gave her best smile. Politics, no matter what country, was politics and Israel's were not a white-glove game. "Of course," she said, "we all trust each other."

Creases appeared on the ambassador's forehead as he glanced at her. He took his reading glasses and began.

"Should I leave?" she asked.

He motioned with his hand to stay. He finished and put the letter inside his coat pocket. Then he took a deep breath. "Anything else you have to tell me?"

"Yes, there are reports that Arab terrorists are trying to buy huge amounts of weapons. Indications are it could be here in England, France, or possibly the US."

"That's not news. We all know that."

She nodded, "That's true, but they sent a particular person who has wreaked havoc with our intelligence agencies. Every time we come close, he disappears."

"Do we have a name, a description...anything?"

"Ahmed."

"That's a big help. If it isn't that, its Mohamed or Nasser."

She ignored his comments. "We do have a description as to height and weight."

"That only narrows it down to several million males."

"There's one other thing." She could feel her face turn red. "On his left cheek of his bottom there is a mark."

"His...?"

"It has a distinct...eh... call it disfigurement."

"And how... never mind, I'll guess."

"Unfortunately, our agent is dead. We can't figure out how."

The ambassador drummed his fingers on the desk. "And that's the second part of your mission?"

"We all keep secrets."

Chapter Twenty-Three

Paris

The morning light slipped through Giselle's blinds and kissed her. She stretched and felt well rested after a night's sleep. Charles Aznavour played on her alarm radio. The coffee with her boss, Inspector Ricard, continued to resonate. It reaffirmed her career was going well. Being his top aide in only five years on the force was an achievement. She had flourished, despite the male-dominated department and chauvinistic attitude of many. Although her looks got her the interview and job offer, it was her brain that moved her forward. Time ticked by. She kicked off the covers. Her step was lively as she hummed with the radio and took a shower. She was going to have breakfast at the Millesime Hotel with an old high school crush. A perfect way to start the day. Her shift didn't start until two.

She arrived at the hotel's restaurant and attracted sideways glances as she waited for the maître d'. A woman always knows. She wore a black dress that tastily revealed her finer points. Her dark luxurious hair hung dreamily below her shoulders and her makeup was subtle but perfect. She could have worn a more informal outfit but *non*. René Neumburg had shunned her once in high school. Today, he would realize what he'd missed.

"Bonjour, madame, would you like a table?" Even at this hour the maître' d was in formal wear.

"*Merci*, I am waiting for a friend. The reservation would be in the name of Monsieur Neumberg for ten a.m.?"

The gentleman ran his finger down the open page. *"Je suis désolé*, I do not see that name. Perhaps…"

"*Non*, may I have a look?" She pointed to the dining area.

"Of course."

She walked by tables desiring to be unobtrusive. The French may have perfected the art of ogling, but she was onto it. Conversations stopped for a second or two as she passed. She returned to the waiting area and checked her watch. It was well past ten. She had a sinking feeling. Was René standing her up? She pushed the thought away. *Impossible.* They had talked all week about this breakfast and how excited they were to see each other. He had some…she didn't remember what work he did, only he was flying from London. *Was this high school all over again?* She took a deep breath and checked off several other excuses, illness, work, a wife? He would have mentioned that. Her high-heeled shoes started to pinch, and it felt warm inside the restaurant. She needed air. Before stepping outside she checked her phone. There were no messages. *Bastard.*

***

Soreil and Karen drove to the Millesime Hotel. On the way they argued over the letter he received that morning.

"We don't know anything about this man," Karen said. "It smells like a trap."

"Could be an opportunity. We could recoup our losses."

"Listen to me. I don't like it. We don't know anything about him or who sent him."

Soreil made a turn. "Details. It costs nothing to find out."

He pointed to the street in front of them. We're close to the hotel. What do you want to do?"

Their discussion became animated. He pulled into the driveway.

"We should wait in the car," Soreil said.

"Nonsense. It could be all day. Besides we will draw attention."

"There's a space across the street with a view of the front."

"Really, Alex, you think no one will notice? Sometimes… I'm going in. At least I can find out if she checked out."

Soreil swung his arm across to block her. "Wait. Isn't that her?"

Karen looked up and saw a woman in a black dress and dark lush hair standing several feet from the entrance. "From the back, yes, I think…"

"No time. Do you have the midazolam?

"It's in my purse with the injector." She opened her bag. The shot was wrapped in foil. "Got it. Do you remember how to use it?"

He swallowed what he was going to say, then took the small weapon.

"Good luck," although her voice conveyed skepticism.

"You're coming with."

"What?"

"Of course. We go together. We have to do this quick." He pantomimed his action.

"No time to argue. Let's go."

"Get her in the back seat," Soreil commanded. *"Vite."*

"I'm going as fast as I can. Do you have the rope for her hands and legs?"

"It's on the floor in the back. See it?"

Soreil got into the driver's seat and as soon as Karen pushed their victim inside, he started the car and pulled away from the curb.

"I haven't closed the goddamn door. Stop."

He hit the brakes and waited until he heard it slam, then took off. "Tie her up good. We can't let her escape again."

"You plunged that needle in the right spot. She'll be out for hours."

"I did, didn't I? Maybe I'll go to medical school when this is over."

"Excusez-moi, monsieur le docteur." Karen bent down. "There's a lot of rope here. Were you thinking we're tying a horse?"

"Just do it."

He checked the rearview mirror and could see only the top of Karen's head. He heard her breathing.

"There. She'd have to be a magician to get her legs out of these bindings." Karen sat up and pushed the victim to the side while grabbing the victim's arms and tying them behind her back. "All done. Amazon couldn't package her better." She seized a handful of the victim's hair and pulled. She let out a gasp.

"What's wrong?" Soreil asked.

"Merde, merde, it's not her."

He turned his head to see.

"Watch the road, damn you!"

He switched back to the highway and searched for a place to stop. "What are you saying? You said it was her…Susan, Françoise…whatever her name. *Foutre,* double *foutre."*

"I said? *Non,* it was you. 'It looks like her from the back.' Stupid. Well, it's not her from the front."

He had to pull himself together. He changed lanes despite the horns from cars he cut off and maneuvered to the side for emergencies. He jammed on the brakes and lurched forward. "Show me her face, Goddamnit." He then turned around.

Karen shoved the victim toward him.

"Sacre bleu. It's not her. Who is she?"

"If she was awake, she'd tell you."

Soreil, on the brink of exploding, fought for calm and let the snide remark pass. Whoever this person was, she was a beauty. Dark thoughts flashed. Could she be used… sold? He knew several disreputable people who would jump at the chance. Karen would never agree. She'd be a problem. But… for enough money… she could come around. Several seconds went by. "Okay, we made a terrible mistake. We can't undo it. For now, in daylight, we are stuck with her."

"We can't go back to our hotel."

"True. What about that farm outside Versailles. It's not too far. Robert, our friend, told us to use it whenever we want."

"Yes, but what if there are other guests. Then what?"

"We can call?"

"And say what? We kidnapped someone and need a place to stay?"

Soreil checked the mirror for police or a stranger who'd stopped to lend a hand. The longer they stayed, the more of a risk. A decision had to be made. *"Bon,* we'll take a ride. If someone is there, we'll leave. By then, it will be toward evening and we can dump our guest if need be."

"Another half-assed plan, but it's better than nothing."

"Sweetness becomes you. Watch her. If she stirs…"

He grabbed the shot he used off the seat. "Use it. There's some midazolam left."

***

Inspector Ricard looked at his watch. It was well past 2 p.m. Where was Giselle? He asked Personnel whether she'd called. The reply was no. This was not like her. At 3:30, Ricard phoned her home. No answer. He tried her cell with the same result. *Is she upset with me? A vacation she forgot to mention?* He tapped his pocket for cigarettes. A nasty habit, even more so since the office prohibited smoking. He debated whether to light it anyway. *Mon Dieu, what is happening. So, she's late. Perhaps she's sick, or god forbid in an accident. I must get perspective.* He put on his coat and went outside. The air was crisp and sunlight flooded the street. The combination felt good. He lit his cigarette with one strike of a match. He had a knack for that. He began to walk in no particular direction. The bookstores, favorite cafés, boulangeries with their intoxicating smells, all ignored. If he'd kept track, he realized he'd walked about ten minutes, 1,000 steps. His wife would have known. Those kinds of statistics were important to her. She'd ask from her sick bed if he got his paces in. *Remarkable what pops into my head.* He stopped. To his surprise he was in front of Kayser, the café he and Giselle were at yesterday. On a lark, he stepped in to see if she could be there. *Foolish. Why would she do that?* She wasn't. He checked the time out of habit. Now it was after four. Two hours and not a word from her. He looked up. The sky was that perfect blue without a cloud to blemish it. The air, though, had changed. Imperceptible, but he felt it. His sixth sense from being a cop for so many years kicked in. His gut rumbled. It was unmistakable. Something was very wrong.

Chapter Twenty-Four

Chicago

"Why are you all giggly?" Shep asked as they left the storage company's office and got into the car.

"Oh noth'n, noth'n. Lordy, I still got the touch," Billy Dee said.

"What in blazes are you yapping about?"

Billy Dee put the key in the ignition and started the car. As soon as they got a block away, he pulled over, then reached into his pocket. "How's this for a picture of Susan Dumond?" He handed the photo to Shep.

"I'll be damned. Never saw you do it." He looked from the image to Billy Dee. "Remind me not to play cards with you. Jesus." He eyed the photo again. "Not a bad-look'n broad."

Billy Dee ignored his partner's observation. "Got to be sharp and quick. Fast hands and clear mind."

"Don't get carried away with that mind bull shit. You got the picture, what are you going to do with it?"

Billy Dee was quiet and concentrated on traffic. He was about to go for the cigar in the ashtray but thought better of it. "Ever been to prison?"

Shep's jaw dropped. "Are you nuts? No, I haven't."

"Don't mean it that way. Now we got this picture, we need our convicted felon, Jack Monte, to identify it as the same person who was in the van with him."

Shep rubbed his face. "Why would the mope want to help us?"

"'Cause there's no statute of limitation on murder. There's still dead bodies and few suspects."

Shep went for his cigarettes but stopped. "I've got a confession to make."

"Yeah? What's that."

"You know how you hate hospitals? Well, I've got the same attitude toward prisons. Can't stand them. Don't like being confined."

Billy Dee took his eyes off the road for a second. "You're kidding, right? I mean they're not my favorite places either, but…"

"Just made that way. I get a bad feeling every time I go to County. Hate the smell, hate everything about it. All these years and we haven't found a better way."

"Watch it, Shep. You're sounding like a liberal."

"Never."

Billy Dee smiled. *Always knew old Shep had a soft spot.*

They were getting close to where his partner parked his car. "Any ideas?"

Shep turned from staring out the window. "I'll look Monte up on the State's inmate app. We'll go from there."

Billy Dee slid his car next to Shep's. "You're all right, my man. The meal is on me when we go."

Shep got out of the car and walked to the driver's side. "Billy Dee, you know the way to a man's heart. I'll be in touch."

He waited until his partner drove off before heading home. He was going over in his mind the next steps to take. Time was short. He had three days before leaving for Paris. Hopefully, Shep would have the information later today and make the arrangements. *Janine won't like it. She'll put up a stink.* He could hear the conversation.

"Why you do'n that for?" she'd ask. "Shep is the police. Have him go. We got so much to do before we leave.

The anticipation of the argument tired him. *You'd think after all this time it get easier and she'd understand.* He took the cigar from the ashtray. Nope, for as long as he'd been married noth'n going to change. For better or worse and some days it be both at the same time. His ruminations were interrupted by an incoming call. He fumbled for the right button to press on the steering wheel. His first try lost the connection. Seconds later, it rang again. Success. The dash showed an unfamiliar number.

"Hello, speak up I can hardly hear you," he said.

"Mon…?"

The caller's voice was scratchy with heavy static.

"Mon…. Jackson?"

"Who?"

"Is this Monsieur Jackson?"

"Mon..yes.. this is Jackson. Inspector Ricard?"

"Oui, I hope it is not too late to call."

Billy Dee glanced at his watch. "Nah, it's late afternoon here. What can—"

"I have some…"

"What was that?"

"Your trip needs to be delayed."

"Say again."

"Yes, there's been a terrible development and your visit must be postponed. I hope you understand."

"I..eh.. yes, of course. When do you—"

"As soon as I, eh, we, get control, I will contact you. Please excuse the inconvenience."

"Sure, sure. I'll keep working on this from my end."

"Merci. Oui, please do. *Au revoir."*

Billy Dee pushed Disconnect. He let the information sink in. Clouds took over the blue skies. It looked like a storm was coming. Soon, raindrops pelted his car, first slowly, then in sheets. Minutes later, it passed as if nothing had happened. He cut the window wipers and turned into his street. Janine ain't go'n to like his news. No sir.

Chapter Twenty-Five

Paris

Inspector Ricard returned to the office from his walk and called Monsieur Jackson, the American retired cop. The conversation was short, and he believed it ended on a pleasant enough note. Then Ricard sent an alert to all hospitals in the area regarding Giselle. Next, he sent an officer to her apartment. He could not concentrate on any other work. He sifted through the papers on his desk without reading them. Every few seconds he'd look from the reports to his telephone waiting for it to ring. A half-hour later, the light on his desk phone blinked. He grabbed it and with much effort fought to control his voice.

"Ricard here."

"Inspector, this is Agent Letrec. I just spoke to the *proprietaire*. She saw Giselle this morning when she looked out her window."

Ricard conjured the image of an old busybody. "Yes, what did she see?"

"She said that Giselle was alone walking in the direction of the metro. She was wearing a dress coat and heels."

"Did the landlady notice anything strange last night?"

"I… I'll ask."

Ricard waited several minutes.

"Hello?" Officer Letrec returned on the line. *"Non.*

Giselle came home around seven and did not leave until the morning."

Ricard doodled on a pad while listening. *"Merci,* Letrec. Go back to your beat… oh, one more thing. What is the landlady's name?"

"Marie Brodeur. I will, sir."

Ricard hung up and stared into space while processing the information. Giselle was going someplace. She was dressed up. She was meeting someone. *Merde. I shouldn't be jealous. I have no claim. Who is he?* Ricard stood quickly and walked around his desk. *Maybe it was a she?* He turned that thought over in his mind and stopped behind his chair. *Non, it was a he.* She wore heels. She was going to meet a man. Ricard pounded his fist into his hand. He was a fool and an old one at that. To think… He flopped into his chair. *Okay, it's not the end of the world. It could be an old friend…a relative, even.* A laugh escaped from him. *I am a goat who sees but refuses to believe what the eyes tell me. Assez. Enough.* One thing for sure, she was missing. He'd drive over there. Her apartment may hold some answers.

Chapter Twenty-Six

London

Jodie left the Ambassador's office soon after she finished her coffee. There was a mutuality of interests between her and Ambassador Vergon. They kept each other's confidences. Regardless of whether it was matters of state or the political intrigues of governmental officials, or the elements of gossip and jealousy… personal matters, none of it went further than the walls of the room.

She was aware that Vergon suspected she knew the contents of the Prime Minister's letter. In fact, she did. Vergon would be replaced soon. Not because he wasn't doing his job. The British press loved him. The Ambassador, having been born in Australia, still had that cheeky accent. But, the P.M. believed Israel needed someone more reliable. Meaning, the P.M. wanted someone who was more in debt to him. Loyalty in this government trumped competence. She, on the other hand, gave the P.M. his due. For the while, even Dovid ben Yamin had to put up with her.

She entered her temporary office, which had a beautiful view of the grounds. There was a small couch, two cheap chairs, and a desk. The walls were painted beige. A picture of a much younger, smiling P.M. hung on the wall. Did Dovid put the picture there as a reminder of her earlier affairs? The thought crossed her mind, but then dismissed it. Dovid was not creative or subtle. She slung her brief-case on the desk and saw the button on her phone console flashing. Who knew she was in London? She grabbed the receiver and pushed.

"Yehudite, this is Joseph. I checked with the Canadians about your friend. There is no Michael Zandular. He died in two thousand-four. Shalom."

***

Paris

Zandular heard the room phone ring as soon as he opened his door. Strange. Why would his handler, Nasser, use the hotel phone? It must be Susan. She was leaving. He hurried and almost tripped over a towel left in the hallway.

"Hello? Su—"

"Michael?"

The female voice on the other end caught him off guard. "Who is…"

"It's Jodie Adams. Remember? Your friend from Ben Gurion Airport."

"J…o…d, Jodie! What a pleasant surprise." He glanced at his watch.

"Did I catch you at a bad time?"

"No…no… I was about to leave for a meeting."

"I won't keep you. I'm flying into Paris this afternoon. I was hoping we could have dinner."

"Din…ner?"

"You sound as if I just asked you to commit a crime. Just thought, you know, two strangers in Paris catching a bite.

He wiped sweat off his forehead with his free hand. "Of course. A pleasure. I do owe you for getting me through that airport. How about seven p.m.?"

"Good. I'll make reservations at Restaurante Georgette. It's about a block from your hotel."

"Georg… fine. I'll write it down."

"See you there. Enjoy your day."

He heard the click and replaced the receiver. He stared at it for a moment, wondering what just happened.

***

Susan glanced at her watch again. Time, she knew, passed differently depending… The wait for Zandular seemed to take forever when in fact it was a little more than five minutes. Even so, she wondered what could be taking him this long.

She stared at her wrists and her mind took her to another place. Jack Monte. Was it a year? Two? He had tied her hands and feet, then thrown her into the back of a van. Time was endless and fleeting at the same moment. The pain seemed never-ending but despite that, she prayed to have another second, another moment of life. She looked at her watch again. A few more minutes went by. Restlessness took over. Her palms grew clammy. Her stomach gurgled. Could Zandular be thinking of… Did he go to his room, not for the passport but for a weapon? Why? What for? Her mind swirled with unfocused thoughts. Then it hit her. Dumond. Her Dumond was a man of charm, but along the way collected enemies. When it was to his advantage, he forgot promises. Deals made were broken. She knew Dumond had that side of him, but not to her. At least… She looked around the room, then checked her watch. No Zandular. Did he know Dumond? Why wait to find out? She stood and went to the maître d' to ask the location of the washroom.

"It is behind the bar toward the entrance, mademoiselle."

"Merci." She walked in that direction and then followed the exit out. She spent the next several hours wandering Paris streets. Toward late afternoon she passed a cab stand and hailed a taxi.

"Millisieme Hotel, *s'il vous plait.*"

"Oui, madame."

Traffic grew congested within a block of the hotel. Several police cars with lights flashing were parked along the curb and in the street.

"I don't think we can get through," the driver said. "Something must have happened."

She thought for a moment, then decided. "Okay. Let me out here." This time she paid. She walked up the driveway and heard someone call.

"Giselle?"

"Who?" She turned. A man who identified himself as a police inspector approached.

The officer stepped toward her then stopped. *"Pardon, mademoiselle,* I thought… I was mistaken. Have a good day."

"You too." She looked toward the entrance of the hotel, then asked, "What happened?"

The officer's eyes were downcast, as if some light clicked off. "We're investigating a possible abduction of a woman. From the description, she was of the same height, weight, hair…and from the back, I thought it could have been… Unfortunately, it's not."

"I'm so sorry. I hope you find her."

"Oui, merci."

✶✶✶

Michael Zandular hung up the receiver. He had a bad feeling that there was more to Jodie's phone call than dinner. He fell into a chair to think. He'd call his handler, Nasser.

The son-of-a-bitch had the contacts to do research on this Jodie Adams. If she came out clean, it could be an enjoyable evening. It not… Done. He went to the closet. The bag wasn't exactly in the place where he had put it, and the zipper appeared slightly opened. Was he imagining this? He opened the suitcase. Everything was in the right place. Although, something felt odd. He had the feeling that the contents had been gone through. *But who? How?* He found the envelope where it was supposed to be, apparently untouched. He opened it and took out the picture Nasser had given him. Yes, he had seen Susan's face before. He smiled. Allah was good to him. She had fallen into his lap and more. He quickly put everything back. He didn't have to pursue the secondary target. He had the primary. He closed up his room. Jodie's phone call was all but forgotten as he strutted down the hallway to the elevator. This was turning out to be the best mission he ever had. The elevator brought him to the main floor. He walked into the restaurant and looked toward the table where they breakfast. Another couple was seated. He glanced around the room, then went to the maître d'. He pointed to the table and asked, "I was with a lady. Do you know where she went?"

The maître d' shrugged. "She left."

No more needed to be said. Zandular moved away from the maître d'. He gave a quick glance through the restaurant just to be sure Susan had left. It shouldn't have happened, but it had. He had fallen under her spell, like a high schooler who needed, no, wanted, more of her. He had pictured the rest of the morning in bed reliving the indulgences of the past night. All because of that damn phone call from… Jodie, or whatever her name. Now, he actually had to work. He glumly recognized this was not a pleasure trip. He had a mission and it wasn't fucking a beautiful woman. He went back to his room. He laid down for a minute, and dozed off. Upon awakening, he glanced at the clock next to the bed. *Oh my God.* It was late afternoon. He kicked the covers off and sat up. How could he have been so careless? He had to find Susan. If not her, then the secondary target. He grabbed at his pocket for his phone. There were no messages from anyone. His breathing calmed. Nasser had given him an address for Susan. It was in the suitcase with the envelope along with her picture. There was still time to at least check the accuracy. He pressed the remote for the TV before going to the closet. CNN's Wolf Blitzer's nasal reporting of the bombed Israeli embassy in London filled the screen. He stopped and stared. The name of the alleged bomber scrolled on the bottom, caught his attention. "No," he said out loud, "impossible, his people can't be that stupid." His mouth went dry. *Were they sending him a message? Your services are no longer needed?* No time for that, he had to leave, now. He grabbed the suitcase from the closet, then opened the safe and retrieved his gun. He stuffed the weapon in his waistband and went to the room's front hallway. He twisted the doorknob but before opening, let go. Instead he looked up and used the peep hole. Seeing and hearing nothing out of the ordinary, he pulled the door a crack then wider and peered down the hallway. He took a hat from his luggage, in case there were cameras, and hugged the outer wall to the stairwell entrance. Leaving hotels by the back stairs was nothing new for him.

Chapter Twenty-Seven

Chicago

"You sure Monte is in Stateville?" Billy Dee asked Shep after getting into the car the next morning.

"That's what it says on the website. And the nice people down there confirmed." Shep pulled away from his friend's driveway. "Does Janine know where I'm taking you?"

"Of course. Why?" Billy Dee looked away.

"She doesn't, does she."

"Man, what are you, my priest?"

Shep laughed. "I can always tell. What did you say?"

"I'm not confessing nothing." He patted his pocket for his cigar.

"No, no, no. My car, my rules, remember?"

Billy Dee stared blankly at him. "This is go'n to be a long ride. Ain't it."

"Don't go south on me, Billy Dee. I'm doing you the favor. You're the one going to Paris. I'm not."

Billy Dee glanced out the passenger window. "Yeah, about that."

"What did you say?"

He faced his friend. "I said, about that. Inspector Ricard called after I dropped you off. Something had happened and he put off the trip."

"No shit." He drummed his fingers on the steering wheel. "Does your wife know?"

Billy Dee shook his head.

"So why are we going to see this mope Monte?"

"I told Ricard I'd work on it from this end. See what happens. I thought about it before dropping off to sleep. If this is the woman, maybe she's also connected not only with the bodies in that house, but that Hugo fellow who had the warehouse on Lake Street."

"What are you talking about?"

"You had an argument with a detective from Belmont and Western. He had Daniel's wife in custody. After you left, I followed the detective that night to a warehouse on Lake Street owned by someone named Hugo. I staked out the place. After the detective left, someone from the inside opened the door. I didn't get a good look. A few minutes later a car shot out from the driveway and passed me. It wasn't Hugo."

"It's coming back to me. Daniels was the lawyer who sold guns to the gangs."

"You're like an elephant. Yeah. Well, Hugo, a day or so before this, was found shot in his bed with his hand on the family jewels."

"Are you saying what I think you're saying?"

"Man, you're like an old IBM computer where you key-punched the information. Susan Dumond may be our new Bonnie Parker."

"Who?"

"Bonnie and Clyde. She was the Bonnie…"

"Don't have to spell it out. Got it. This is getting more and more complicated." Shep reached for a cigarette.

"You're not…"

"Like I said. My car…"

"Oh shit." Billy Dee hit the lever to open the window.

***

The entrance at Stateville was medieval. Despite the well-kept lawn in front, the admittance building was gothic in style and towered over the flat plain. Barbed-wire laced the perimeter and guard towers were in plain sight. This was the Big House, the end of the road for many. The structures were meant to scare the hell out of you.

"Hate this place. Hate it, hate it," Shep said. He and Billy Dee walked from their parked vehicle. "Maybe you go ahead. I'll wait in the car."

"Come on, Shep, you're the one with the real badge."

Shep winced. "Damn."

***

Versailles

Giselle groaned as she regained consciousness. She had no idea whether hours or days had passed. Her mouth felt it had a dozen cotton balls stuffed inside. She tried to move her arms and legs. It came as a shock and then terror when she couldn't. *What is happening?* She felt the sensation of movement but couldn't fathom why. There was only blackness.

A mixture between a scream and moan escaped her. She didn't have the energy to open her eyes. Darkness. Her heart pounded. Nausea rose from her stomach and stuck in her throat. She told herself to focus, but she was cold one minute and sweating the next. She gasped for air. In this chaos she felt someone or something touch her shoulder and lower neck. Seconds later her skin was pricked. Her world went spinning and she floated to a sun burst of colors.

***

"That should take care of her for another few hours." Karen removed the needle from Giselle's neck. "I'm even better than you. It's not easy to administer a shot in a moving car while the bitch is thrashing."

"Bravo to you," Soreil said, "you can be called doctor, too."

Karen glanced at her slumped-over prisoner. She was definitely pretty despite the drool and the paleness of her skin. The bitch would make any man happy, maybe women too. Today, what was once no is yes and vice versa.

In Tunisia, a woman like her prisoner would fetch a handsome sum. Kidnappings, particularly in villages, happened frequently. A runt of a man would inspect her body like a horse-flesh buyer. He'd poke, comment, then make an offer. That began the negotiation. The bargaining would be between him and another male. The centuries-old custom was very much alive and well.

"Honey, you can't hear me," she said to the knocked-out captive, "but at least you were lucky this didn't happen there."

Karen moved away from her and looked out the window. She searched for a road sign. "We should be close."

"About thirty kilometers should do the trick," Alex said.

Karen looked at her watch. "Twenty minutes. What happens when we get there?"

"Leave it to me."

She stared at the passing scenery. His words none too reassuring.

* * *

Stateville

Billy Dee and Shep emptied their pockets and were

searched each time they went through different security stations. They knew enough to have left phones, keys, and other accessories in the car. At each of the checkpoints, their identifications were examined and the same questions asked as to why they were there. Each time they explained. Security demanded them to open the file envelope they brought and made them remove all staples from the papers. Guards checked the list of visitors for that day at each escorted checkpoint. Needless to say, time was not important for those in charge. The wait at each stop seemed to take longer the closer they actually got to meeting with the prisoner. After about an hour, they were led to a room and told to wait. The door slammed with a click.

"Nice," Shep said. The room was about ten by nine. "Just what I always wanted, to be locked up with you."

"Hold on, it could be worse," Billy Dee said.

Shep flashed him a look. "How's that?" He stretched his arm to check the time, then remembered security took his watch. "Don't even know the hour of the day anymore. I bet it's afternoon. Well past lunch."

"We can always order a baloney sandwich from the commissary."

"Funny man. How long before they bring the mope?"

Billy Dee sighed and grabbed one of the plastic chairs. "Look at this. The damn thing wobbles."

"In case you didn't know it, we're not at the Hilton. Everything here stinks. What's more, I don't like being locked in a room. It gets to me."

"Calm yourself. At least we'll be out of here after the interview."

"We better be."

Chapter Twenty-Eight

London

Jodie put the phone down after her conversation with Zandular. His reaction to her was less than enthusiastic. That may mean nothing; after all, she did call out of the blue. Was her Israeli chutzpa showing a bit too much? She noticed a gardener brushing dirt off the sidewalk. A gardener, now? She watched for a few moments, then her thoughts drifted back to the phone call. At least he remembered who she was. It may just come down to men. He could have found a new shinny object. A guy like Zandular would. That's how he operated. That's how he found her. If he was fearful of being discovered, the last thing he'd do, even if he knew who she was, would… A movement caught her eye. A group of people walked toward the spot where the gardener had swept. *Oh my God.* In an instant the glass from her window shattered. Shards flew through the air. She dropped to the floor. She wasn't cognizant of the explosion, but her ears were plugged and rang with a high-pitched sound. She yawned, then did it several more times to get her ears to pop. Thank God the desk blocked most of the destruction. She got up on her knees and touched her face. Blood covered her hand. For an instant she wondered whose. Reality then sank in. She stood, using her other hand for support. The outside air rushed in. She saw uniformed people scurrying in all directions. Body parts were strewn over the lawn. She stumbled out of the office. Chaos was in the hallway…men, women, shouting, running. Someone jostled her as they went by and she slipped. That was all she remembered. When she woke, Herschel Joseph, the security attaché sat across from her. Her hand went to her face and felt a bandage.

"What happened?" she asked.

"Another suicide bomber." He looked away.

"What is it?" She grabbed his sleeve.

"I'm afraid Dovid is no longer with us. He died in the blast."

She wanted to cry. She wanted to scream at the unfairness, the continued persecution. It would be for another time. "Anything left of the bomber?"

A small smile edged around his craggy face. "We have enough for an identification. The bastard actually set the bomb off by remote. We fingerprinted and used DNA."

"You have a name? An identification? Who was the bastard?"

He nodded his head, yes. "It may be hard to believe but the bomber came back as Michael Zandular."

"What the…" She said it so loud that she felt the stitches on her face stretch. "I was on the phone with him minutes before. It can't be. No, it can't." Tears flowed down her cheeks. She grabbed Joseph's hand and squeezed.

***

Paris

Susan entered the Millesime Hotel after having been stopped by an officer minutes before. As she made her way to the bank of elevators, she eyed the TV screen hanging over the bar. She stopped and stood at the entrance. The picture showed the aftereffects of the bombing at the Israeli embassy in London. She couldn't make out what was said, but there was no mistaking the name that flashed on the screen. *Sacré merde.* She continued to stare at the TV. It could not be. It must be a mistake. She wanted a drink. She took a step toward the bar, then stopped. She could hear Dumond advise her. "Not the place." She felt dirty, in need of a shower. To think she made love all night and into the morning to that... She had to disappear... again, like Chicago after she freed herself from Jack Monte.

✳✳✳

Stateville

A loud click turned Billy Dee's attention to the door. Seconds later, a guard entered the room. He searched both Billy Dee and Shep. It was only then that another guard brought Jack Monte. The prisoner wore shackles on his legs and hands.

"We'll be outside," said one of the guards.

"You again," were the first words out of Monte. "I have nothing to say. Where's my lawyer?"

"How you do'n, Jack," Billy Dee said, "have a seat."

"Fuck you."

Shep, who was standing, balled his fists.

"Easy there, Shep. Jack ain't use to civilized company," Billy Dee said. "Why don't we all grab a chair."

Shep hesitated, then sat.

Monte gazed around the room and finally did the same. "What do you mother-fuckers want?"

"Nice of you to ask. We're all doing fine," Billy Dee said. "Getting down to business, we're still investigating the murders at that house along with the arms dealer Hugo."

"I ain't say'n noth'n without my lawyer. I'm not a fool. No more freebies, assholes."

Billy Dee could feel the tension well up in Shep. He knew Shep didn't have much love for Monte. "Listen, Jack, we're not stupid. We know you have rights. All we want you to do is to identify a picture."

Jack let out a laugh. "A picture, you say. What kind of picture?"

"It's a photo of a person." Billy Dee reached into the file for Susan's photograph. "Was she the one in your van?"

"Bring it closer. My eyes aren't as good as they used to be."

Billy Dee held the photo closer.

"Yeah, that's the bitch, all right. She killed the other woman in the house and did Hugo too."

"You sure?"

Jack smiled. "The dead bitch was very much alive and doing me. The one in the picture ran into the room and swung a hammer that cracked the bitch's skull. Am I sure? The bitch wasn't moving so good after that. She didn't move at all. I was fucking the daylights out of her but didn't finish. As for the cunt in the photo. I would have fucked her too, but didn't get the chance. She did me so wrong. In the van she admitted shooting that other guy. What's his name? Eh, Hugo. I hope she burns in hell."

Billy Dee put the photo back in the file. "Guess we're done here."

"Hey, what do I get for help'n you out?"

"An extra baloney sandwich from the commissary," Shep said as he stood to alert the guards.

Chapter Twenty-Nine

Paris

Inspector Ricard stood in the driveway of the Millesime Hotel in the late afternoon. He watched as the woman he stopped went inside. *This is what happens when hope overcomes reason.* Now that he thought about it, there was a resemblance to Giselle. Perhaps it was the light, and the approaching nightfall. Shadows misconstrued. He sighed… but it was slight. He reached into his pocket for the note he found in Giselle's apartment. It was in her handwriting. "Millesime Hotel, 10:00 a.m." By the time he reached the hotel, all the day shift workers had left but for the maître d'. The manager pointed him out.

"Bonjour," Ricard said, introducing himself. "I'm with the Paris police." He flashed his badge.

The man took a step back. "Monsieur, what can I do for you?" He looked from Ricard to the manager.

"I'm looking for a woman. She had a reservation for ten this morning."

"I'll be happy to check the book. Just a minute." He walked off to the restaurant. A few minutes later he returned. "This is the list of reservations. Take a look."

Ricard put his glasses on and ran down the names. *"Non,* she does not appear."

"Désolé. For some reason we were very busy."

"Maybe she was waiting for someone who had the reservation?" He opened his file and pulled out a picture.

The maître d' studied the photo. He held it with one hand while the other brushed through his hair. *"Non,* I can't say." He returned the photo. "I wish I could be more helpful, but…" He shrugged.

"Merci." Ricard put the photo back in the file. He turned to leave, then had one more thought. "She wore a dress coat and heels. She is quite attractive." Ricard felt his face flush.

The maître d' knitted his eyebrows. "Attractive? Inspector Ricard, many of our guests fit that description. I have a wonderful job."

Ricard thanked him again and began to walk away.

"Just a minute." The maître d' went toward him. "There was a woman, quite… you know… who was waiting for someone. She asked if a reservation had been made. After I looked and told her no, I believe she left."

"Do you remember the name of the person and the time?"

"I know it was after ten. The name? No, but if I think of it, I will call."

"Merci." Ricard left the hotel.

***

Versailles

"She's stirring again," Karen said, looking over at the prisoner. "The stuff should have knocked her out for hours."

"The farm is just up the road. We'll be there in a few minutes," Soreil said. He peered in the rearview mirror. The woman squirmed, then groaned. She was still under but he knew not for long. He remembered that the highway forked, but wasn't sure whether to go right or left. He chose right. Within, a half of kilometer, he knew that was a mistake. It took another kilometer for him to turn around. Of course, Karen made a comment about his lousy sense of direction. He tried to ignore it as well as the increased noise from the back.

"She's waking," Karen said.

"I can hear." He searched the road for the cutoff. There. Fermes de Robert, the small sign read. He turned. The lane wound around batches of trees, then pastures. A cow interrupted her eating and stared at their passing car. Up the road went, until the house came into view.

"Do you see any cars?" Karen asked.

"Non, the parking is in the back." He slowed to a stop. "I'm going to pull off and walk the rest of the way."

"Uh-huh, and leave me with…her?"

"Just so I get the lay of the land. Can't drive up, then turn around if someone is there."

"What do I do with her?"

Soreil reached under the seat and took out a club. "Use it if you have to."

***

Karen held the weapon across her knee and watched as Soreil's figure disappeared toward the house. "You better not wake," she said. "I don't want to bash your pretty head." Whether her prisoner heard or not, Karen didn't know, but she quieted.

The car grew uncomfortably warm despite Karen's window being partially lowered. She opened her door and stepped out. It felt good to stretch her legs. She walked up the road a bit, wondering if she'd catch sight of Soreil. She was at least fifty meters away when she sensed movement. She turned and thought she saw the prisoner sitting up. *Merde.* She broke into a run, remembering the club was on the floor of the back seat.

***

Giselle opened her eyes. It took her a few minutes to realize she was in a car and it had stopped. Her body felt as if a thousand-pound weight was on her. Questions swirled in her head. Where was she? How? Why? The last thing remembered was walking out the hotel. She realized she was on her side. She could see the door handle a millimeter or two from her face. She knew her hands and legs were tied, but she wasn't gagged. For some reason, she felt not exactly pain but heat run from her neck to her shoulder. She tried to sit up. It took several attempts to succeed. She was breathing heavily, and sweat from her forehead ran into her eyes and stung. To her surprise, she saw the door on the other side of her was open. She looked out, then in front. She was alone. She struggled to remember what she'd been taught at the police academy. Did she sleep through that lecture on how to get out of this sort of jam? Or did she daydream about the officer who explained the steps one needed to take? *Think.*

***

Soreil reached the crest where he had a clear view of the house. He avoided the paved road and stuck to the dirt path that led to the back. There were no cars. He was in luck, for a little bit, anyway. He felt no need to investigate further. It was more important to return to Karen, or so he thought. With each step from the house he imagined his conversation with Karen when he'd meet her at the car.

"The caretaker could be inside. Why aren't you more careful," she'd say. "You don't think."

The imaginary talk got him angry. It was so real. She had changed. She no longer admired him. Once, he walked on water; not anymore. Once, he could make love to her anywhere, anytime, and she not only complied, but was a full participant. Now that desire was met with scorn. He kicked a stone out of his way. When? How? He automatically touched his pants pocket. When he was rich, and had money, she was…

Dumond. He changed all that. Lose the money, and you lose the woman. Simple, not complicated at all.

The house was barely visible. He switched from the path to the gravel road. It twisted and turned, heading downward. There were trees on either side of him, and below he saw the car and pastures. As he got closer, he saw a woman running toward the vehicle. He took his gun from his pocket and picked up his pace. It happened so fast. From his distance he saw the woman near the passenger rear door.

"Stop!" he yelled. "Stop!" And at the same time he fired.

✳✳✳

Paris

Ricard returned to the station late that evening. The strain of Giselle's disappearance reflected in his mood. He had spent the hours chasing down any tidbit of news, but still had nothing. He marched through the hallways without stopping to chat with other officers. His face, he was sure, reflected his "not in the mood" for small talk. His goal was to reach his office and shut the door. Only then could he reflect on Giselle's disappearance. He was a few feet from his destination when Officer Abbé called his name. He stopped and although his patience was thin, waited until she hobbled from the computer area to him. Ricard had once been told by…he couldn't remember, that Abbé was once the belle of the ball. Officers fell over each other for her. Well, time had done her no favors.

"Oui," he said in an exasperated voice.

"This came for you over the fax. It's from Chicago."

"Chicago?"

"Oui," she said. "Chicago, as in Etats Unis."

He took the papers from her. "I know it's in the United States." He mumbled a dismissive *merci,* and went into his office, closing the door behind him. He dropped the papers along with Giselle's file on his desk, then hung his coat. He went to his cabinet drawer and reached in the back to retrieve a bottle of twelve-year-old GlenDronach scotch. He looked at the bottle for a second or so to admire the color of the liquid. Its cost was a bargain compared to others in its class. He uncorked the top, then poured some into his coffee cup and took his seat behind the desk. *Chicago. Americans should only know the French drink more scotch than cognac.* "To Giselle," he said softly, as he raised his cup, and took a sip. It tasted as good as it looked. He put the drink down, then moved the fax papers to another part of his desk and opened her file. All he knew was she went to the hotel to meet someone. Who, was still a mystery. Did that person show? Did she meet him outside? He picked up her photo that was next to his notes. *Where could you be?* He sighed. He needed to interview the day crew at the Millesime and wished he had been able to, but... information comes in slowly. Hopefully it would not be too late. He took another sip and his whole body relaxed. He reached for the faxed papers. It was from the ex-cop, Billy Dee Jackson. He put his glasses on to read. His heart raced as he turned to the second page and stared at the photo. It struck him. He quickly compared that one with Giselle's. The resemblance was unmistakable. *Mon Dieu.* He realized she was the person he'd seen at the hotel. He grabbed at the first sheet and reread it. Jackson connected the photo to a name.… Susan Dumond. Dumond? His gaze fell on the huge file that gathered dust on his desk… the murder of Eduard Dumond. He sat back and let the facts play out. Could this also be the same person Giselle identified as Simone Dubois, the weapons dealer? He gulped down the last of his drink, then slammed the cup on his desk. He had to go back to the hotel…tonight.

Chapter Thirty

Paris

S usan didn't go into the bar. Instead, she took the elevator and went to her room. She grabbed the few items she'd purchased during the day and stuffed them in her newly bought overnight bag. She took the stairs to the main floor and slipped out the back. A quarter of a kilometer later she hailed a cab. Besides a drink and a shower, she needed a place to think.

"S'il vous plait, Les Deux Magots," she said to the driver. As soon as she said it, she realized her mistake. That was where she ran into Soreil and that woman Karen. They could be there…waiting. *"Excusez-moi,* I meant Le Refuge Café, on rue Lamarck."

The driver looked at her. "That is in the eighteenth arrondissement, on the other side of the river."

"Oui."

He looked at his watch. "My shift is almost over. Les Deux Magots is an excellent café, mademoiselle."

"Oui, but I'm exploring new places."

He shrugged. "Of course." He then said loud enough to hear, "What do the young know," and drove off.

Twenty minutes later they pulled up to the café. She paid the fare. There were tables on the outside filled with people who sat under heated lamps. She could also see the inside and hear the noise of the larger crowd. She picked an outdoor table in a corner with a view of the entrance. She noticed the café was tucked in between two sets of stairs leading to Lamarck-Culaincourt train station. It was Parisian quaint. Within a minute or two a waiter brought a menu, dropped it on the table and left. *So much for charm.* The renown Gallic attitude was on full display. She did a quick review of the offerings and decided on a glass of chardonnay, when and if the waitstaff returned. Another five, ten minutes went by before a staff member came back.

"Will there be anyone joining you?" he asked.

"*Non,*" Susan replied.

His look was one of regret. Possibly because the check wouldn't be so large or a waste that she was dinning alone. *C'est la vie.*

He stepped toward a table of four without taking her order. "Pardon," she said stopping him. "A glass of…"—she eyed the list quickly—"Vouvray."

"Very well. Anything else?"

"*Non.* I'll start with that."

He scribbled on a notepad and without a smile left. She watched him disappear into the inside throng. She sighed and took in her empty table. If only… if only. Dumond? Please, we wouldn't be in a corner watching the world pass by. No, he'd converse with those next to him, and those behind him. His laughter booming. Soon, he'd invite everyone to join, and after rounds of drinks and food, he'd gather her up and leave. The night's affair picked up by others. Money wasn't an issue with him. He always seemed to have it or know where to get it. She, on the other hand… The waiter returned and plopped her drink on the table. "*A votre santé,*" he said.

"*Merci.*"

"Will there be anything else?"

"No…n…eh …*une tasse de soupe à l'oignon.*"

"A cup of onion soup. You said it like a Parisian."

"I am a Parisian. And you, sir, have the slight accent of the south of France, *n'est-ce pas?*"

The waiter put his pad down. *"Très bien.* What place?"

"If I guess right, is the soup on you?"

He looked toward the sky for a moment. "Only if…" A smile covered his face. "You have dinner with me later tonight."

She looked at him in a new light. He was tall, dark hair, his face rugged but kind. "Deal. You are from the area around Bordeaux. *Oui?"*

He picked up his pad. "I will take the soup off the check."

Her smile had no effect. He walked away. *Men. They slink off when a woman bests them. "Cochon,"* she said under her breath, glaring at the empty space where he had been. She took a sip of her wine. She shouldn't get distracted. There were more important issues…like dwindling finances, the bomber in London, and the Zandular of last evening. *Were they the same?* Then there was Soreil and Karen. Those two. *Who are they? What do they want from me? Is there a common thread? Dumond?* The possibility seemed fantastic, but the more she thought about it, the more possible it became. Dumond and his enemies. She took another drink. The reality of that proposal settled in. Everything that had happened to her in the past few days was a setup. Somehow Soreil and Karen knew she would be at Les Deux Magots. They let her steal his wallet. *Sacré bleu,* she never saw it coming. *Dumond, you were a devil.* She remembered what he once told her: *"Every plan has a surprise. Adapting is surviving."*

The waiter returned with her soup and set it down. "I'm off in a few minutes. Here is your check."

He was all business. His face gave no hint of wanting anything else. She dug out a ten-euro note. "Here, *bon soir."*

He nodded and left.

She watched him. *It is better this way. Another man, another bed, another headache.*

***

It was late afternoon in Paris. The day would soon fold into night. The streets full of Parisians and tourists rushing home to make dinner plans. Zandular easily blended into the throng. According to his handler, Nasser, Susan had checked into the Hotel de France Invalides under the name Simone Dubois. His first instinct was to hail a cab, but then he thought otherwise. The metro would be more discreet, but there were cameras. He was familiar enough with Paris to know that the hotel was close to three kilometers away. The walk would do him good. It would allow time to figure out what to do. His route led him to the rue de Babylone, which passed the Eiffel Tower. He'd seen it many times and it still held its magic. He interrupted his thoughts to gaze on it like the multitude of tourists around him. After he got his fill, he continued on, pondering his situation. First, he had to obtain new ID. His passport was an invitation for the flics to arrest him. That led to the next question. Did this happen because of the dead girl in Israel? Was Jodie's phone call from London a cover for that? His concentration was momentarily interrupted by a beautiful woman whose shoulder nearly brushed his coat. Her figure lingered in his mind until it was erased by other questions. Why did his organization use his persona name for that of the London bomber? Zandular is not like John Smith.

Logically, Nasser would be the man with the answers. He should call him. So simple but yet, complicated. His cell phone could be traced. That left a pay phone… if there were any, or the use of someone else's cell.

He had a new thought. Men as well as Allah moved in mysterious ways. What if Nasser had one hand visible and the other hidden? A plan that Nasser did not tell. He, Ahmed, had served the organization well. He had done what was asked. He believed in the cause. Was it possible that could be held against him? He murdered that Israeli girl on their orders. He took no delight in it. It was a mission. Got the information about gun emplacements. The penicillin was a novel way to dispose of her. He got the job done.

Lost in his own debate, he carelessly bumped a couple laden with packages. They were wrapped in Bon Marché department store paper, now strewn across the walk.

"*Excusez-moi*," he said, "how stupid of me. Let me help you." He stooped to the sidewalk side by side with the woman and picked up the fallen items. "Please forgive me. Lost in thought…you know."

The man helped the woman up, then eyed him. "Next time, sir," he said in English, "a little less thinking and a little more seeing."

"Yes, of course," Ahmed said. "I'll do that. *Bon soir*." He watched the couple disappear into the crowd. Tourists. He resumed his walk, with his hand in his coat pocket, gripping the woman's cell phone.

Chapter Thirty-One

Stateville

Jack Monte was placed back in his cell after his meeting with the two detectives. He was good at not showing his anger, but it was there. Those cops made a fool of him. Especially the one named Billy Dee Jackson. He could do without the other either, detective… Shep, if that was his name. The dumb fool that he was, helped those two dicks and got nothing for it. But it was the picture of that bitch, Susan, that made him seethe. If it wasn't for her, he'd wouldn't have been caught…shut in like a caged animal. He'd be out there, eating, drinking, fucking…living. He believed in the cause of a free Serbia. He was part of their liberation army as long as they paid. He had murdered, bribed officials, and smuggled weapons for them. At least he did, until…Chicago. He failed in that one, but they still owed him. The SLA should have reached out to him by now. They should have helped him escape. Instead, there was only silence, except for one visit by a Mr. what was his…Stan…some…kovic…Stankovic. He promised him a lawyer and money for his well-being. In return, he was to say nothing. A lawyer did show up, a Mr. Drovik, and through Drovik's efforts, he landed in prison for many years. So much for his help.

Monte sat on his bunk for a minute, but then got up

and walked the perimeter of his cell…back and forth. An idea began to form. Before his arrival in Chicago, he'd been in Paris. It was he who set up the murder of Dumond. It was he who, acting as a paramedic, arrived at the scene and took Dumond's remains. He discovered a great deal from the papers and keys he stole.

He learned where Dumond stayed through hard work and luck while preparing for the old fox's demise. Once he obtained the key, and dressed in a flic's uniform, Dumond's apartment was easy to access. He found a treasure trove of information, especially about Susan and her mission in Chicago. She was the one sent to obtain the weapons. He also found addresses that he presumed were safe houses for either Dumond and/or Susan. If he lured Susan back to Chicago, the cops with his help would nail her for the murder of the woman in the house on the far south side, Hugo, the weapons dealer, and perhaps others.

Darling Susan. She would look so… so chic in an orange jumpsuit. He tapped his tongue against the roof of his mouth and made a clucking sound. A waste of a beautiful body, but in prison, someone would surely benefit.

He stopped his pacing and stared through the bars. His hands clutched them until his knuckles turned white. All this for a price. He laughed. Freedom.

***

Chicago

The ride from Stateville took longer coming back than going. Stopping for lunch may have had something to do with it. Time slipped by as Billy Dee and Shep commiserated over their years with the Department. In between swapping stories, Billy Dee munched his way through a burger and chips. Shep had roast beef piled high on French bread with mayo dripping down the sides.

Billy Dee gazed at his friend's sandwich. He argued with himself about speaking out, thought better of it, and continued to watch his friend eat. After Shep took two or three bites, Billy Dee couldn't contain himself. "How many times have I told you. That," he pointed to Shep's sandwich, "goes with hot mustard, not mayo. It's like pouring ketchup on a hot dog."

"You eat it your way, and I'll eat it mine. This is America."

Billy Dee grunted and returned to his meal. When the bill came, true to his word, Billy Dee paid. Shep, in response, ordered a slice of key lime pie. It took another five minutes for the waitress to bring it.

Shep took a bite, then another. His face lit up. "Pure joy."

"You done?" Billy Dee pointed to his watch. "I've been gone almost all day. I needed to be back hours ago."

"One more bite. I should get a refill on the coffee." He looked at Billy Dee. "All right, you won't let me enjoy the full ambiance of it. Let's go. For the record, you owe me."

"What?"

"Hey, not my fault your wife will be upset. Not only did you sneak out and visit that mope in jail, but you haven't told her about the other small detail."

"Don't you start. Let's move."

***

Shep turned the corner onto Billy Dee's block.

"I'm going to fax the picture of Susan and a brief synopsis of Monte's statement to that Inspector Ricard," Billy Dee said.

"Knock yourself out. You're still no closer to Paris."

Billy Dee gave Shep the eye and held the file a little closer.

They drove up the driveway and stopped.

"I see the missus is on the porch waiting to greet you." Shep waved and rolled the window down a bit. "Afternoon, Ms. Jackson." They both nodded. Shep turned to Billy Dee, who had opened his door. "By the look of her, you're in trouble."

"Let me worry about that," Billy Dee said. He paused for a moment before getting out, then leaned into the car. "I know the way to the doghouse… I built it." He shut the door and waited for Shep to back out before he stepped toward his front door. He had a foot on the stoop when Janine went toward him.

"Why, Billy Dee, you remembered the address? I'm not go'n to ask where you been gallivanting all day. No, that ain't me. I don't interfere with your business. You a grown man, you knows all that you should know."

"Now Janine, I…"

"Get in the house. We got neighbors."

"Yes ma'am." Billy Dee brushed passed her and got a step into the hallway before he heard the door slam.

"Billy Dee, somethin' wrong with your expensive phone. It didn't work all day. Ain't that a bitch. All that money you spent, and nothin'."

"Janine, this is an iPhone. My phone work fine." He realized by her glare that was the wrong thing to say. "I…I mean…"

"You mean? What you say'n is you ignored all my calls and texts."

"It ain't like that. Shep and I went to the…"

"Billy Dee, we've been married a long time, don't bring Shep into this. I'm an understand'n woman, but Shep ain't go'n to cover for you."

"Janine, it's not like that. We went to Stateville, for the case in Paris."

"Say what?"

"If you hold on, I'll tell you everything you want to know."

She took a seat on a living room chair. "I'm listening."

He explained to her the connection Susan may have with the murders and the SLA gunrunners. She nodded and let an occasional "ah hah" escape from her. When he finished, he told her he was going into the kitchen to get a beer. A few minutes later, he returned with a bottle and took a swig.

"It taste mighty fine," he said, falling into the couch. "See, baby, I had to keep the phone off, going into the prison and all." He got the feeling he said the wrong thing again.

"It still don't explain why you kept it off."

He clutched the bottle a little tighter and played for time by taking a drink. "You right, baby, I guess I forgot."

That was met by a louder "ah-huh." Janine got up from her chair and came closer to her husband. "Billy Dee, I've known you a long, long time. I know when you ain't tell'n me something. Now, I bought everything I need for our trip. It all laid out on our bed. You go'n off to Joliet two days before we're to leave don't play right. You not answer'n the phone…no sir." She shook her head. "What did you leave out, Billy Dee?"

He wished there was more beer. He wished he had a case of it. *There is no gett'n around it. She'll have to know.* He cleared his throat. "Well, I may have left out somethin'."

"Yeah? What?"

"That Inspector called me. You know, the one from Paris."

She had her hands on her hips. "I know who you talk'n about."

"He said there were some issues, there, and the trip… the trip had to be postponed." He heard his wife gasp.

"I need to sit down."

"He didn't say it was cancelled, Janine. Just put off until, you know, whatever the problem was is taken care of."

Janine almost stumbled to her chair. "All dem clothes and shoes I bought. What am I go'n to tell our friends?"

"Noth'n," he said getting up. "Tell them nothing. None of their business." He headed toward the door to the basement.

"Where you go'n?"

He understood his words broke her heart, but what could he do? "Listen, Paris is still on, only delayed. I'm faxing papers to that Inspector. This could be what's needed to get the problem solved on his end."

"Lord, pray that it is."

Chapter Thirty-Two

London

Jodie let go of Joseph's hand, then brushed stray hair out of her eyes. "I'm a mess." She looked around the makeshift medical room in the Embassy and saw others being bandaged. Blood everywhere. She took a deep breath, "It's all a mess, Joseph. It will always *be* a mess." She took a deep breath. "Is the Ambassador all right?"

"As far as I know. He got held up on a call. He was supposed to be with Dovid."

"*Baruch Ha'Shem,* thank God. What time is it? My watch, who knows where I left it."

Joseph looked at his phone. "Almost one, why? You going somewhere?"

She smiled, then let it vanish. "I thought Paris would be nice after a terrorist attack."

"Paris? Are you crazy?"

She focused on his face. "You know me by now. To do this job, we all are a bit crazy." She looked around the room and observed the controlled chaos. People moaning, medical personnel shouting. "I'm done here, let's go."

They stopped several times on their way out to wish the injured well. She recognized the Ambassador's secretary who, moments before, was it only minutes ago, was full of life and energy. Now, she was bandaged and lying on a cot. "You will be okay," Jodie said.

The secretary glanced up, acknowledging Jodie's presence. *"B'seder,"* she said, short for variety of meanings of "okay, it's in order."

They squeezed out of the room. In the hallway, they avoided the paramedics and embassy personnel all shouting, running, but taking care of the damage. "You see, Joseph, even when there is chaos we go about in an odd sort of order."

They walked out of the Embassy and stood outside the front door. "Paris?" Joseph asked. "You think your Zandular is part of this?" His hand swept the grounds of the building.

"Don't know. What we do know is his name is not Zandular. He could be connected to this, or Shoshana's death in Tiberias, or he's the agent in search of weapons. Any of the above or none. That's why I have to go. We can't afford more innocent lives lost."

Their eyes locked for a moment. "Okay, I'll make the arrangements," Joseph said. "What time do you want to arrive?"

She told him of her dinner plans with Zandular. "I want enough time to check into our Paris Embassy, change, and get to the restaurant fashionably late. I'll also need a hotel room."

He looked like he was going to say something, but instead shrugged. "Whatever it takes" He let out a breath."

"B'seder."

***

Paris

"Who is this?" Nasser asked.

"It is Ahmed." He glanced around the area of the wooded garden to make sure no one watched.

"I don't recognize this number. I'm hanging up."

"Don't. I called three times."

"There are many Ahmeds. How do I know it's you?"

"Please, it's me." He pointed to his chest although Nasser couldn't see. "I stole this phone. I can't use mine because of London."

"Praise be Allah. The Israeli… prove who you are or I hang up."

"Nasser, doesn't my voice sound like me?" No response. Ahmed looked up to the sky. *"Allo,* you still there?"

"Yes, but not for long."

"Okay, okay. You had a wife. She…eh…died about three years ago, at the Hadassah hospital in Jerusalem. You believe the Israeli doctors killed her. I was the cab driver who drove you home. That's how we met."

"Yes, yes, you are sounding like Ahmed. What else?"

"What else? You are unshaven and a bit overweight. You like…no, you love mansaf, lamb with yogurt, but it must be tender. Should I go on?"

There was static then, "You are making me hungry," Nasser said. "Have you accomplished your mission?"

"Yes and no."

"Which part yes and which part no?"

"I found target one, but because of London, there is a problem."

"A problem?"

"Yes. My cover name."

"I don't understand."

Ahmed held the phone away from his ear and stared. The feeling Nasser wasn't the brightest was his kept secret. Nasser, it seemed, was only a messenger, an order taker. "Nasser, the bomber's name was the same as mine. Zandular is not the Arabic version of Mohammad or the English, John Smith. There aren't many of them."

"I don't see the problem. The bomber is dead. You're not. Allah will provide. Finish the job."

"Na…hello… you there?" He stared at the phone and recognized the call was over. *Merde. Idiot. Can he be that stupid?* He swallowed and sorted out what he should do. The cell was still in his hand. He had to get rid of it. He looked around. The trees and shrubbery hid him well.

He smiled at the irony. He was standing on the grounds of the official residence of the French Prime Minister. Hidden off the rue de Babalone were two camouflaged doors that led to this magnificent garden. The Gardens of Matignon were open on certain days to the public. Today was one of them, but it would be closing soon. He checked again that no one else was near as he wiped the phone with the sleeve of his coat, then tossed it into the shrubbery.

***

Susan didn't realize how hungry she was until she began to eat her *soupe à l'oignon.* The deliciousness of it made up for the waiter and the haughty service. The melted cheese on top spilled over the sides. The baguette had a crunch even though it floated in the onion broth. Between the soup and the wine, Zandular was almost forgotten. She played with the idea of dessert, but that would require service from a staff that operated on the "less was more" principle. She tore off one more piece of bread and wiped the bowl. *C'est fini.* She got up and went to the side of the café's entrance. She positioned herself so that she could see the inside, but would not be seen. The crowd of diners had thinned so that she had a good view of who remained. She gazed around the room and didn't see Karen or Soreil. She moved away from her spot. Zandular…if he was still among the living, she doubted he had the ability to find her. She was safe for the moment. But as Dumond had often reminded her, safety was relative.

She knew Dumond had places all over the world he'd called safe houses. It was an occupational necessity for him. She was aware of some but not all. There were also certain hotels that for the right gratuity placed the guest "off the books." Using her phone, she searched what was near. The Hotel Des Arts was less than a kilometer. *Was that one of them?* There were too many hotels and too many rooms to recall. She rubbed her forehead trying to remember. She could picture the scheme. Dumond had her stand to the side and accentuate her chest while he negotiated. "Say nothing," he instructed. The blurred images of countless clerks who deftly glanced at her, then turned to Dumond, washed through her mind. She smiled at what they must have thought. Sometimes they were right. *Alors,* she would get a good night's rest and then figure out what to do. Too much happened in the day.

The male hotel clerk did not look familiar, and there was no Dumond. It was all on her. Before she went to the desk, she undid the top button of her blouse, then slung her overnight bag over her shoulder. There was a natural pulling apart that gave anyone who looked a peek.

"Bon soir," she said. *"Je voudrais une chambre, s'il vous plaît."*

The clerk glanced up. He was well trained and hid his leer well. *"Certainement,"* he said, checking the computer. He asked all the routine questions of how long she'd be staying and the room she desired. *"Bon,* I will need a credit card and identification."

She leaned forward, and slid three 100-euro notes toward him. *"Pour vous,"* she said, and put a finger to her lips.

He hesitated. His eyes went from the money to her face and then her front. His hand swept the cash toward him. *"Merci,* here is the key."

The room had a view of Studio 28, a cinema for *filmes d'art.* She closed the shade and sat by the small desk. A copy of the *New York Times International Edition* lay folded on top. Unlike Dumond, who had been a voracious reader of newspapers, she read the news from her phone. If she read it at all. Politics and the like did not interest her.

Dumond often chided her for that flaw. "To stay ahead, you must learn the politics of the place. What makes it tick. Who is doing what to whom."

He'd say that line, while he unbuttoned her blouse with the TV on in the background. She'd laugh. A surprised/ hurt look would come over him, as if her laughter was unexpected, misplaced, but the gleam in his eye never left. Afterward, while they lay together, he'd say again, "Read. There may be useful information hidden in those columns of stories."

She picked up the paper and browsed through the articles. In the third section, there was a headline that shocked. "The Serbian Liberation Army—Is it Alive and Well?" She felt a slight tremor in her hand as she read the column. Near the bottom of the article were three paragraphs about what took place in Chicago. It described the death of several people, among them a Dragon Petrovic, a vegetable vendor/weapons dealer who went by the name… Hugo. His murder, the writer said, "was still a mystery."

She dropped the paper on the desk. There was only one person who thought he knew who the assailant was in Hugo's murder. Only one…Jack Monte. She took a deep breath, went to the bathroom, and turned on the shower. When she finished, she dried herself and stepped into the room. She pulled back the covers of the bed and got in. Her mind fought sleep. Faces of persons crowded out the yearning to fade to oblivion. The last thing she remembered was Dumond's voice. "Safety is relative."

Chapter Thirty-Three

Paris

Inspector Ricard opened his office door while struggling to put on his coat. The personnel in the room looked up from their desks. He could tell from their eyes their dismay as to what the hell he was doing there, so long after his shift.

"*Bon soir,*" a chorus of them said as he passed by.

He nodded, then saw Officer Letrec coming into the room. "Anything new with Giselle?"

"*Non,*" he replied, "it's a mystery. There's not a trace of her. Nothing from the hospitals in the area, either. We've placed a car near her apartment, but so far…" He shrugged.

"*Merci,*" Ricard said. "I may have some new information." He patted his front pocket. "I'm going to the hotel again. Come with."

Letrec's eyes widen. "My shift…"

Ricard swung his gaze to the large clock on the wall. "Yes, yes, you're off duty in a few minutes. Understood. Have a good night."

Ricard walked out of the station. This was the new police. Everything was by the clock…union rules. This was France. A plague on the rules. A person's life…one of their own… He shook his head. His school, his way, was fading, a life that would no longer exist. Change came along whether one liked it or not. He got into his car and for a fleeting moment thought of going home. *What's the use?* Giselle's image pushed that idea away. *If there's a chance…* He turned the key and the engine roared. The tires squealed as he pressed the accelerator. The surge of power felt good. It gave him a sense of control over an uncontrollable situation.

The Hotel Millesime was lit up, as it was every night. Ricard slid his car up the driveway. The doorman was immediately at his side. "Otto" was engraved underneath the hotel's lettering on his coat. Ricard opened the door and flashed his badge. "Please park it on the side. I don't think I'll be long."

"*Oui,* Monsieur l'Inspector."

He took a step toward the entrance, then stopped. "Just a minute."

He caught Otto's attention just before he pulled off with the car.

"Oui?" he said.

Ricard took out a picture of Giselle as well as Susan. "Have you seen either of these women?"

Otto studied the photos. "May I?" he said, reaching for them.

"Of course."

Otto brought the images closer to his face. He turned the photos slightly.

"Well?"

"I'm afraid not, Monsieur l'Inspector. Are they sisters?"

"*Non,* they are not related."

Otto shook his head. "Remarkable," and handed the pictures back to Ricard. "Perhaps the day shift. I started at seven p.m."

"*Merci.*" Ricard waited to let Otto drive his car past him before heading toward the entrance and into the hotel.

"May I see the manager, *s'il vous plait?*" he asked at Reception.

The smile on the young woman's face disappeared. It was replaced by a furrowed brow and a concerned voice. "Is there a problem?"

"Non," Ricard said and took out his identification.

"Oh." Her voice went higher. "I'll see if Monsieur Arnolt…" She looked down at her switchboard. "I'll get…" She dropped the receiver in her anxiousness.

He reassured her that she and the hotel were not in trouble. "I am looking for two women." He took out the photos. "Have you seen either of them? One, I believe, is a guest. I believe I saw her earlier late this afternoon."

She looked closely at the pictures. *"Non…*I don't… maybe… This one," she pointed to Susan's picture. "She… what's the name?" She turned to her computer.

"She may be going by Dubois, Simone Dubois."

The receptionist typed in the name. *"Non.* Could she have used another?"

Ricard scratched his head. *Another? Must be. Did Giselle tell me another name?* "I'm not sure," he said. "Have you seen her?

The woman gazed at the picture again. "Monsieur Inspector I very well may have, but I… wait." She picked up the photo. "Monsieur, I… I think she booked a room with us two days ago. Yes, she said she was going shopping for clothes. She was very attractive." Her face turned a shade of red as she pointed. "I am sure that was her."

"What name did she use?" Ricard kept his voice steady although he felt a surge of adrenalin.

The color went out from her cheeks. "I…I'm sorry. I don't remember."

He bent over the counter to better view the computer. The screen was dark. "Have you seen her this evening?"

"I don't think so."

"What time did you start?"

"After nine p.m. I was supposed to be here at six, but I called Monsieur Arnolt and told him I'd be late."

He hoped for a better answer. "Who covered for you?"

"Henri. He left when I came. I don't think he was happy with me."

"Oh." He was sure his disappointment was plastered on his face. The day had been too long. It's time…

"Henri," she called, "Henri."

Ricard turned and saw a young man with blond hair leaving the bar area. He stopped and walk toward them.

"What now? Isn't it enough I worked—"

"Henri, this is Inspector Ricard." She didn't wait for further introductions. "Did you see this person?" She held up the photo.

"Yes," he said after two seconds. "She waved a hello, then I assumed she went to her room."

"Which room?" both Ricard and the young woman said in unison.

He sighed, then shrugged, "I don't know. I remember, though, her name was Françoise…Fran…Lebanese started with a B."

The receptionist's hands went flying over the keyboard. "Here it is. Bélut, Françoise, room four-oh-three."

A thousand questions flooded Ricard's mind. How did this Henri know? He eyed the young man, then keeping his excitement level, pointed to the phone. "Please call."

The receptionist picked up the receiver. "What should I say?"

"Tell her the cable is bad and you are sending a service person."

She let out a nervous laugh, then dialed. He heard the clicking sound from the connection. It must have rung a dozen times. "No answer," she said.

He sighed. "Do you have a key?"

"Monsieur l'Inspector! I cannot," she said.

He was about to argue, but Henri intervened. "I'll go with him."

There was no conversation in the crowded elevator. They reached the fourth floor and Henri led the way, their footsteps muffled by the thick carpet. Outside room 403, Ricard asked Henri to knock. No answer. He knocked with the same results. Ricard nodded to Henri, who inserted the key and opened the door.

"Allo," Henri said entering. "Mademoiselle Bélut?"

Ricard followed. The bed was made. He checked the drawers and the closet. They were empty. He stepped into the bathroom, and there was no evidence of anyone being there. Even the garbage cans were clean.

"Are you sure this is the room?" Ricard asked.

Henri's face was flushed. "Yes, that is what the computer said."

"Did she check out?"

Henri's stared. "Non, Monsieur Inspector, it looks like she skipped out."

***

Versailles

Soreil kept his hands outstretched in the shooting position as he moved toward his car. He focused on the woman lying outside the rear passenger door.

"Karen," he yelled. "Karen?" He quickened his pace. As he got closer, he could tell by the clothes and form that it was her. He sucked in air and swore at a God he rarely mentioned. He dropped the gun on the hood and kneeled beside her. "Karen, answer me."

He pushed her over so that she would be on her back.

Her front was covered in blood. He grabbed her wrist and searched for a pulse, although as Karen would often remind him, he had little medical ability. "Where is your goddamn pulse? What should I do?" He went farther up her arm. He felt nothing, then glanced at her face…lifeless. "No, you're not dead. Come on, stop fooling around."

She didn't move…no smile, no backtalk, nothing. He stood and stared at her. "Idiot, why did I…" He threw his head back and shouted at the sky. "It's you, you did this." God didn't answer either. He walked several paces away from her and swept back his hair. An emotion he never expected went through him. Grief…tears. He wiped his face. Were they for her, or him? All those years he'd had with her. There was fun…excitement. They grew into an old married couple who weren't married. He sighed. What was done was done. He kicked a stone from under his shoe. He was alive. His life would continue. Prison was out of the question. His legs felt shaky as he turned back toward Karen. His gaze went from the body to the car. Movement. The driver's side rear passenger door flung open. A woman, his captive, sprang out and ran.

***

It may have been minutes or seconds after Giselle realized she was alone in the car. The rear passenger door was open, and she heard someone approach. No more thinking of what to do. She flung herself, stomach down, on the seat, lifted her arms behind her as high as they could go, and while twisting her hands, pulled down. Her limbs hit her backside and the rope loosened. She wriggled her hands free. She sat up and leaned over to untie her legs. She heard a boom…then another. She sat up. Gunshots. Someone screamed, then footsteps. A male voice. "Karen…Karen?"

Giselle glanced quickly at the opening, then worked to untie herself. She undid the last knot. She looked toward the open space. There was a man at the far end of the open door. Their eyes met for an instant, not a word said. Giselle leaned into the driver's rear passenger door and released the lock. She ran.

Chapter Thirty-Four

Chicago

Billy Dee slouched in his basement chair as he heard the fax machine send his papers to Inspector Ricard. *How does that little thing do it? In seconds, the photos, my report … Paris.* He shook his head. *Damn amazing. Couldn't figure out how if I tried. A bunch of numbers and whirls. Lord have mercy.* He reached for his bottle of beer, then remembered he left it upstairs. He needed time to relax. It had been a long day. Prisons, jails, never bothered him before. He understood the system. Hell, he had been part of it. His job for a long time was to make sure those in his jail were safe. What happened afterward, guilt, innocence…well, maybe not innocent, that was someone else's problem. But waiting to see Monte…was a whole other story. Can't move without being told. Can't do nothin'. Once inside, either as a visitor or prisoner, someone else had control. He shivered, but he wasn't cold. Man, I'm gettin' soft or old or both. Pretty soon I'm not only hear'n Shep, but I'm gettin' to be like Shep.

"Billy Dee, whatcha do'n down there so long?" Janine asked.

Her question interrupted his thoughts. "Noth…fax'n papers to the French guy."

"You send'n a book? You've been there a long time."

"Naw. I'll be up soon."

He heard her move away from the door. Poor Janine.

She did have her heart and everything else set on this trip. Hell, even he was excited, although not like her. She always wanted to see the world. He'd be happy in front of the TV watch'n sports. Well, marriage was compromise. He could watch TV in Paris.

He retrieved his papers from the fax and glanced at Susan's photo. *Nice look'n woman.* Then it hit him. Monte. He checked his watch. Shep may be sick of him but… he had to call. Whether Paris or Chicago, Susan Dumond would be found.

*****

Paris

Ahmed walked out of the Gardens of Matignon and headed toward the Hotel de France Invalides. Perhaps Nasser was right. The London bomber Zandular was dead. He had nothing to do with him. Coincidence. He worked that idea, like trying on a new coat. The dead Zandular was unknown to him. His disguise, on the other hand, was of a respectable Canadian businessman. As he walked, he grew more confident in the cover story. The sleeves fit. He held out his arms to inspect and confirm. Was it perfect? He admitted probably not, but it would do.

The Hotel de France Invalides faced the massive dome of the Hotel des Invalides. Paris, as Ahmed observed, could not escape the architecture of the Sun King, Louis XIV. He wondered if his masters would provide for him as Louis did for his soldiers. In his heart he knew the answer. But, he rationalized his reward, if there was to be one, was not for this world but the next. He still believed in the cause. There was no place for Jews or a Jewish state on Arab land. Allah had said.

He saw the hotel was up the block. Since he joined the cause, he had become a man of the world, though. He had travelled, and read history. What if Allah was wrong?

He climbed the few steps that led to the entrance. The doorman opened the door. He nodded and went to the area for check-in. Nasser often told him, "Doubt corrupts the spirit. Believing requires less thought and more heart." For an agent, that was still good advice. Success of any mission demanded a 100% commitment. Any less, and mistakes were made. He waited his turn for the receptionist. She was a young woman whose red lipstick was pronounced. Her hair was brushed back. Her perfume was as noticeable as her lips. The nametag that hung from her blazer pocket read Louise.

"Bonjour," she said. *"Votre nom?"* She was poised over her computer ready to type.

He grinned, "Non, not for me. I'm to meet a friend who I believe is a guest."

"Bon," she returned an agreeable smile, *"son nom?"*

He hesitated and went through his pockets. "Eh, Susan... Susan... *Excusez-moi."* He searched for the information that Nasser had written. "Ah, here..." He took out the envelope. "Dumond. Yes, Susan Dumond."

Louise's pleasantness turned from spring to fall. "Monsieur, you don't even know her name." Her gaze was now wintry cold. "I'm not allowed to give information regarding guests."

He nodded. "I, no...no" He gulped some air. "My boss... he..." His phone began to vibrate in his pocket. "Just a minute."

"Monsieur, would you mind moving, so I can attend to the others behind you?"

He held up his hand in a motion to wait, as he answered his phone. "Allo?"

"Michael, it's me. Did you forget?"

"Wha... oh, Jodie." He checked his watch. It was a half past seven.

***

Chicago

"This is a collect call from an inmate at the Illinois State Penitentiary. Do you accept the charges?" the automated voice asked.

"Shep?" Billy Dee, not fully listening, looked at the caller ID. The number displayed was not his friend's. Who the hell...

The automated voice repeated the question regarding acceptance of the call. "Press one to accept. Press two to hang-up."

Billy Dee sat back in his chair. How did any of the mopes have his cell? His mouth went dry as his finger hovered over the #1, then #2 digit. What if it... He pressed #1.

"Thank you," the automated voice said, "you'll be billed at fifty cents a minute." There was a series of clicks, then a male voice.

"Hello?" Billy Dee's hand wrapped around his cell, his eyes glued to his watch.

"Detective Sheppard?"

"No, it ain't Detective Sheppard. Who is this?"

"I mean Detective Jackson. This is Jack Monte. You came to see me earlier, and I identified that bitch's photo."

"I know who you are, Monte. What do you want?"

"I have more information you may be interested in."

"Yeah?"

"Yeah, I do. I could be of great help to you and your investigation."

"How so?"

"Well, I...eh… Detective, everything said is recorded. It would be better if I saw you in person."

Billy Dee's gaze went toward his desk. *What am I stepping in?* "Let me think on it, Monte."

"No problem, but time is ticking."

The line went dead. *What the hell does he mean by that?*

Chapter Thirty-Five

Versailles

Soreil looked away from Karen's dead body and into the back of his car. The woman he kept prisoner stared at him for a split second, then bolted. *"Arretez!"* He took a few running steps toward her, but realized she had too much of a lead. He ran to the hood of the car, his chest heaving for breath. "Stop."

He raised his gun. She was about 50 meters away—almost half a soccer field. She slowed for a second while turning to look. He fired and missed. *"Merde."*

He jumped into the car and steered in her direction. A barbed-wire fence stopped her escape. He pulled the car close to her. She hobbled a distance, then put her hands in the air.

"Don't shoot. What do you want from me?" she asked.

He got out and pointed the gun at her. "Keep your hands in the air. It's unfortunate for you that I got here when I did. You think you could murder a woman and walk away?"

"What are you talking about?"

Her voice did not shake. Nor did she seem scared.

"I'm calling the *flics,*" Soreil said.

"I am the police," she said, and lowered her arms to shoulder height.

"What?" His gun hand shook. He took a half step back. "Stay where you are."

"I am an officer with the Paris police. My identification is in my purse, if you would have looked."

What did Karen do? Didn't she search the bag? Merde. Beads of sweat dripped from his hairline. He dropped his gun arm to his side. "Don't move." He looked over his shoulder and peered into the back seat. "What purse? I can't see it."

"It must be on the floor."

He looked directly at her. "Likely story." He raised his gun arm again.

"If you kill me, you'll be murdering a police officer."

"Shut up." He took a deep breath. "We'll return to Karen. Move."

"*Non,* I'm not going anywhere."

"Yes, you are." He fired. The shot didn't hit her but made her flinch. "You won't be so fortunate next time. Do what I say." His hands were no longer cold. He took in the scene. At another time this would be a different story. A beautiful, disheveled woman stood with her hands raised against the backdrop of rolling hills. She, in a black dress torn at the sides. Her hair flowed in the breeze. Was it a lover's spat? Did the man with the gun catch his mistress in the act with a rival? What a script for a French romantic comedy. Yes, it could be a movie. He spat. But it wasn't. Her life was no longer hers....cop or no cop. Either she'd soon join Karen in eternal bliss... He squinted and motioned with the gun. He kept a prudent distance as she walked slowly to where Karen lay. Her body even under duress swayed. What a waste to shoot her. She could be worth a small fortune to one of his disreputable friends. If only he had a way to recapture her without killing her.

"Kneel beside the body."

She hesitated. "If you're going to shoot me, I'd rather watch my executioner. I want my face etched in your memory—"

"*Tais-toi!*" He raised the gun.

***

Paris

Ahmed let seconds pass before responding to Jodie. "Yes, yes, of course… dinner. I am so rude. I should have called. But…" he sighed, "business."

The number of people around the receptionist spilled toward him. He cupped his hand over his mouth and inched farther away.

"I'm already here, and the chair across from me is empty. I can have another scotch… or two." She giggled.

"Another…" Her features flashed before him. He visualized her curves. "You may have to have three before I can get there."

She laughed. "In that case, we'll skip dinner and go for dessert."

A middle-age man and his wife stood too close to him. Ahmed glanced up from his phone and gave them an icy stare. They stepped away, mouthing their apologies. His imagination went back to picturing Jodie. "Three scotches?" He wondered what the effect would be. He smiled despite himself.

"You'll have to join me to find out." She read his mind.

The conversation moved too fast or, maybe, he sensed too easy. Then again, it had been an ugly day. Susan had disappeared. A bomber by his same name had blown up the Israeli embassy in London, but now this Israeli Jewess was all but throwing herself at him. *What to do? Should I resist?* He heard her soft breath through the phone. It was becoming an intoxicating web. He was about to speak when her naked image vanished. Instead, Nasser's voice rumbled through his head. *"The second target may still be at the Hotel Lutetia. You need to find him."*

"Hello, Michael? Are you still there?"

Her words returned him to the present. "Yes, Jodie." He cleared his throat. "As much as I want to, tonight is impossible. Let's save the three scotches for another time. I'll call. How long will you be in Paris?"

"I've heard that line before, Michael. I'm disappointed." She paused. "Usually that's said after…shall we say, dessert."

Ahmed gripped his phone tighter. Her blonde hair flashed before him. "Well…" He swallowed. "I mean it. I'll set up dinner. Your choice, just not tonight."

"Okay, I'm flying out in the morning, but I'll be back in a day or two. I'll let you know."

"Sure. Good. We'll meet then. Sorry about this evening."

"I am too… very…sorry."

The conversation ended.

"Monsieur?"

Ahmed looked up from his phone and turned quickly. *"Oui?"* It was the receptionist, Louise.

"We have no Susan Dumond staying with us." Her face showed spring.

He nodded. *"Merci,"* and left.

***

Versailles

"Lie with your face on the ground. Feet toward me," Soreil said

She hesitated.

"Vite, if you want to live." He cocked the gun.

She turned slowly, her back to him. A small gust of wind blew and kicked up her dress. Her knees buckled. She dropped to the ground and lay flat with the right side of her face planted in the dirt. He saw her body tensed…

waiting. He pressed his knee into her back. He heard a slight whimper as he placed the barrel of the gun touching her left side. "Don't do anything stupid." With his other hand he pulled out the small vial of midazolam and syringe he had used on her at the hotel. There wasn't time to check what was left. He pressed his knee to her neck.

"I need air."

He quickly filled the syringe and plunged it into the spot where his knee had been. Her body twitched. He put the gun in his waistband, then leaned on her shoulders with his hands. Within a minute, he saw her eyes close and her breathing become shallow. He ran a hand down her back and squeezed her ass. She would more than make up for the money lost with Dumond.

He went back to the car, started it, then parked close to her. In the back seat as well as on the floor, he found the ropes. Lying next to them was her purse. He reached in and found her wallet and held her ID. It read Paris Police Department across the top along with a picture of her in uniform adjacent to her name, Giselle Arrote. He swallowed hard. He was already well down the road to hell. Karen was dead, and he'd kidnapped a flic, then tried to kill her. *A story sensational, oui?* He grabbed the cords and stepped out of the car and walked the few steps to her. There was nothing more to do but go forward with his plan. This time her bindings, unlike Karen's work, would not come undone. He tied her ankles, then ran the same rope to her hands and bound them behind her back. From there he strung the rope to her head and wrapped a noose around her neck. He made sure the line from her ankles to her hands to her head was taut. If she tried to move, she'd choke. His next problem was where to go. Paris was too dangerous. He glanced up the road…the farmhouse. It seemed empty, hopefully for a few days. He leaned against the car and checked his pocket for a cigarette. Nasty habit, Karen would say, but… it no longer mattered. He'd bring Giselle into the house, then bury Karen. He took several puffs, exhaling slowly. It may be nasty, but it was pleasurable. He grabbed his phone from his pocket and along with it felt an envelope. He uncrumpled the paper and read the note within. It was signed by a M. Zandular. Somehow this Zandular believed he could provide weapons, although the request was not specific and between the lines. Where Zandular got that idea, he didn't know, but guessed… Dumond. There was a phone number beneath the signature. God or the devil smiled upon him. He checked his watch for the time. He'd call later that evening.

Chapter Thirty-Six

Chicago

"You know what today is?" Janine asked.

Billy Dee put aside the morning newspaper and looked at his wife. "Well, if yesterday was Sunday, today gotta be Monday. I know it ain't your birthday or our anniversary. I give up."

"It outta your mind already. I can't believe it. The other night you went around the house say'n sorry honey, don't you worry, but a day goes by and noth'n."

"You mean Paris? Christ. I can't make that Frenchman say 'come on over.' I've tried."

He picked up his cup of coffee and took a sip. "However you do it, this is great stuff. Better than any Paris…what are they called?"

"Who?"

"Those make'n the coffee in places like Starbucks."

"Baristas."

"Yeah, better than anyone of them." His compliment had little effect. He put his cup down. "I'm goin' to keep my promise to you, Janine. I mean it."

She took her napkin and blew her nose. "Thank you, Billy Dee. I know you'll try. I do give you a hard time. It's just…" Her eyes welled. "Silly me." She touched her husband's hand. "I'm along for the ride, after all these years."

"That's my girl. Shep and I are go'n back to Joliet to talk with this mope. It could be a long day."

"Shep drive'n?"

"Nope." He smiled when he said it.

***

"I ain't gett'n in the car until you put that damn thing out," Shep said.

Billy Dee took a long puff on his Macanudo cigar. "Get in, don't be a wusp."

"Hey, you need me more than I need to go on this joy ride back to Stateville."

"Weren't you the one who said, 'my car, my rules'?"

Shep held the passenger front door open. "I may have said it, but I'm not going all the way to Joliet with you smok'n that thing."

"All right, you just a big baby. I'll put it out." He took a few more draws and then placed it in the ashtray.

Shep slid into his seat.

"Happy?"

"I'd be joyous if you tossed it."

Billy Dee glared at him. "You're worse than Janine. I ain't throw'n a ten-dollar cigar out the window, not for nobody."

Shep took out his wallet. "Here's a sawbuck. Dump it."

Billy Dee glanced from his friend to the cigar, then snatched the bill. "You win."

***

The interview room at the prison differed little from the other day with the exception that there was a table and three plastic chairs. Monte was led in as before, handcuffed and legs shackled.

"Anything you need, just holler," the guard said on his way out.

As soon as the door closed, Monte leaned back and grinned. He appeared to have all the time in the world. His gaze went around the room.

"What are you look'n at? Noth'n in this place is different." Billy Dee followed Monte's expression.

Shep squirmed in his seat. "Okay, you got us here, talk."

Monte answered Billy Dee but kept his gaze on Shep. "No, you're right and wrong. Everything is about to change."

Shep stood. "I smell a con. I'm outta here. There's noth'n to discuss."

Billy Dee motioned with his hand to sit. "I don't think you're in a position to call the shots."

Monte rubbed his face between his cuffed hands. "Maybe, but I have information that could put that bitch…Susan Dumond…into your grasp." He looked from Billy Dee to Shep. "I see I've caught your interest."

"Go on," Shep said, "but I have a short attention span."

Monte cleared his throat. "I identified her picture and you boys were nice enough to thank me. But I can do more. I can deliver her. I can get her back to the States."

"You can?" Billy Dee asked.

Monte looked straight ahead. "First we discuss the deal."

"You want a get outta jail card." Billy Dee said.

"You have brains, Detective. Yeah, the accommodations here aren't the best and the food is even worse. As for this jewelry…" Monte moved his handcuffed arms and shackled legs. "Not my kind of taste."

"We need details. Besides, it isn't up to us."

"I'm not stupid. I know that, but you can talk. If those in power buy it, I'll get you everything you need."

"Uh-huh, so let me get this straight. You help us get Susan

Dumond, and we get you your walking papers. That's what you say'n?"

"In a nutshell."

Billy Dee caught his partner's look. "How?"

***

Paris

Ahmed left the Hotel de France Invalides and stepped into the night. His mind was still on Jodie as well as Susan's disappearance when his phone rang. He feared temptation would surely overtake him, if it was Jodie. He was several meters from the hotel's entrance when he stopped and looked at the calling number. It certainly wasn't Jodie. Susan? His heart beat a little faster. His hand hovered over the Accept button. What if it was the police? Indecision, but if it was her… He pushed it and heard a male voice.

"*Bonjour.* Monsieur Zandular?"

The voice was unexpected. Certainly not what he wished. He took a second or so to gather himself. "*Oui? Qui est-ce?*"

"You sent me a note about a business proposition."

"A business… oh, Monsieur Soreil?"

"*Oui.* I'm interested but there was a lot unsaid in your note."

"I know. Can never be too careful."

"True. I'm in Versailles, I'd like to meet. Your message intrigued me. I'm certainly in that business as well as…and I may have something that intrigues you. Are you looking on behalf of yourself or…"

"Monsieur Soreil, it's best to talk in person. Okay. Tomorrow… in the morning?"

"Morning…morning. *Oui, bon.* What model car will you be driving?

"Car?"

"Auto, I don't like surprises."

"Certainly. Who does? It will be a Peugeot."

"Sedan or coupe?"

"Ah… does it matter?"

"For identification. If you're renting make it a sedan. The country roads can be trying."

"Country… Where precisely are you?

"I'll text the address in the morning. Say about ten. *Au revoir.*"

Zandular stared at his cell. Definitely this Soreil was not with the police.

Chapter Thirty-Seven

Paris

The night turned cooler as Inspector Ricard left the Hotel Millesime and waited for Otto to bring his car. He gazed at the twinkling lights of the streets, and the not too distant Tour Eiffel. At times, it was a sensuous sight. This was Paris, after all—the city of lights. Tonight, though, all he saw was darkness. Giselle and this Susan of many names were somewhere hidden by the blackness that illumination didn't pierce. Did one's disappearance have to do with the other? He chuckled. God enjoys his games. He gives us air to breathe, and then sits back and watches. We must be wonderful entertainment.

"Your car, Monsieur l'Inspector," Otto said, holding the driver's side door.

"Merci." He had one foot inside but stopped. *"Excusez-moi."* He took his billfold from his coat pocket and gave Otto a five-euro note. "If one of your coworkers saw this woman, please call." He showed him Giselle's picture again. "Keep it. Let me know."

"Of course. *Au revoir.*"

Ricard looked at the time. It was well past his shift. There was nothing more to do. He wondered, as he drove home, if Otto meant what he said, or was his response out of politeness. What's a stranger worth? Otto only saw

Giselle as beautiful, he didn't know of her kindness, that she was smart, dependable. He pictured her at the office as he caught her smile. He tightened his grip on the steering wheel. It was life's cruelness that some unforeseen hand had forced him to play a hideous game of hide-and-seek. A contest where the rules have yet to be revealed. What if… He pushed the thought of her death away. He could not allow himself such negativity. His mouth was dry. The usual bottle of water kept in the car was empty. He swallowed despite the scarcity of saliva and urged himself to focus on the positive. If she was dead, she'd have been found. Non, she was alive, somewhere. Maybe this Susan was mixed up with Giselle's disappearance. His memory flashed back to when he showed Otto the two pictures. Otto thought they were sisters. Ricard drove along the highway, his hand now drumming, as he grasped for ideas. If Giselle was kidnapped, perhaps whoever did it was fooled too.

It was a little after midnight when Ricard put the key in his apartment building door. He picked up the mail from the mailbox in the vestibule, then climbed the stairs to the apartment. Once inside, he placed his coat over a chair and went into the kitchen. There were no sounds other than the ones he made. He went to a cabinet where he kept liquor. His wife would scold him as to the amount accumulated. "Do you think you're a baron? We don't have the luxury of an estate for all the cognacs and scotches."

On nights like this, when he was troubled by a case, she'd stumble out of bed and join him at the kitchen table. It didn't matter the time. Her response was always, "I heard you come in and *non,* I just went to bed."

He knew it wasn't true, but it was lovely to believe. "Ah, Maddie." He said his wife's name as he poured two fingers' worth of Tesseron cognac into a glass. "It would be nice to have you here. I'm in a fix." He stared at the amber color for a second or two, then raised the glass and inhaled the slightly sweet aroma. Only after his senses awoke did he take a sip. The liquid immediately warmed him. As he drank, he explained the details of Giselle's and Susan's disappearance to his departed wife's empty chair across from him. There were no questions or interruptions. When he emptied the glass, he put it in the sink and shuffled toward the bedroom. It was nearly one a.m. He was about to place his phone on the night table when it went off. The ring startled him. *Who would be calling?* He looked at the screen and didn't recognize the number. *Giselle?*

"*Allo,*" he said as calmly as he could.

"Inspector Ricard?" the male voice asked.

"*Oui,*" his response tinged with disappointment.

"This is Otto, from the hotel."

"Otto? *Oui,* yes, Otto."

"*Excusez-moi* for the late hour, but I may have something of interest."

"Please, go ahead."

"A guest told me she was out for her morning run. As she left the hotel she saw a woman standing off the driveway. She wore a black dress. The woman seemed to be waiting for something or someone. The guest walked to the street and a blueish color vehicle drove up and stopped near her. A couple stepped out and whisked the woman into the vehicle."

Ricard felt his heart race. He shed his fatigue and concentrated. "Otto, did she identify the picture?"

"I showed it to her. She said it was possible. She didn't at the time think there was something wrong. There was no screaming or fighting. It seemed the woman just went with them. It was only much later when she saw the news on the television that it occurred to her that she may have witnessed a crime."

Ricard paced around the bedroom. "Did she remember anything about the car?

"She wasn't sure if it was a van or a car. It happened quickly, but I have her name, Mademoiselle Stephanie Cook, room 1217. She said she would be expecting your call."

"*Merci,* Otto, I can't thank you enough. *Bonne nuit.*"

***

Ahmed hailed a cab as soon as he had some distance from the Hotel de France Invalides. He directed the driver to take him to the Musée de Montmartre in the eighteenth arrondissement. It was far enough away from La Villa Madame as well as the Hotel de France Invalides.

"The musée is closed, Monsieur," the driver said.

Ahmed smiled. "It is not a problem. I want to see the building and walk the area filled with history."

The cab started to move. "Monsieur, the whole city is historic. Is there something particular…"

Ahmed got the feeling the cabbie was referring to other things besides architecture. "*Oui,* that is true," he said after a moment, "but on a night like this, the city is most beautiful from the heights of Montmartre."

"You have been here before?"

"Only for short visits. Twice."

Ahmed saw the whites of the cabbie's eyes flicking from the front window to the rearview mirror. *Most likely trying to decide what is my game. Am I into women, men, boys? Who the hell walks around a museum at night?* "I'm an architect by trade," Ahmed said, "and the museum has an intriguing design."

"If you say so."

The taxi pulled up in front of the building and Ahmed paid him well. "*Merci,*" Ahmed said, "*bon soir.*"

The driver grunted his appreciation and pulled away.

He waited until the cab's taillights faded in the distance to begin his walk. He saw the lighted sign of the Café des Deux Moulins a few meters up and realized he hadn't had dinner. This was as good a place as any.

He was told by the waitstaff as he drank his after-dinner cognac that there was a nice hotel just up the way. It was the Hotel des Arts.

***

Susan drifted out of sleep, awakened by what sounded at first like claws of a cat on wood. She opened her eyes to blackness. It took her a few seconds to remember she was in a room at the Hotel des Arts. The scraping noise changed to an identifiable soft knock that became more incessant. She fumbled for the lamp switch, and finally found the chain. The knocking persisted.

"Allo? Who's there?" She grabbed a sheet to wrap around her naked body and moved toward the door. *"Allo?,"* she said again.

"It's Maurice. The one who did you a favor," he said, keeping his voice low.

"Who? What?" She brushed a strand of hair from her face.

"Open the door. I'll explain."

"Open the door? Are you crazy?"

She heard him chuckle.

"Remember your request…off the books."

She had a sick feeling. This wouldn't have happened with Dumond. This Maurice would have been punished… severely. "I paid you well for your troubles."

"Oh, *mademoiselle,* not well enough. Pretty women like you know money is never adequate. I could not afford you any other way."

She leaned on the wall by the door. "You can't afford me now."

"We'll see. Open the door."

"I'm calling the police."

"Not a problem. You're not registered, remember."

She stayed silent.

"I have a key, you know," he hissed.

She took a quick step; her feet entangled in the sheet. She tripped over it and fell into the door. Her hand quickly grasped the lock and realized she forgot to use the chain. She could hear herself gulp air as she gripped the metal ball. Her hand shook so, she dropped it and the chain clanged against the door. At almost the same moment she caught the sound of keys jangling, then another male voice. She gripped the handle and tilted her head so that she could hear.

"What is all the ruckus?" the male voice asked.

"Oh, I'm so sorry I disturbed you. This guest complained of… no heat… and I was… I came up to see… anyway, all is good. *Bon.* She found the switch."

"I have an early appointment and need to get some rest."

"No problem, I will make a note of it and adjust your rate, Monsieur…"

"Zandular."

"Oui, Zandular. Bon nuit."

Zandular? Merde, can't be. She must have misheard. Was that possible? Out of all the hundreds of Paris hotels, thousands of rooms and floors, he was here, if not next door, down the hall? She moved slowly to her bed and plopped down. "It cannot be," she said again. "Impossible, one in a million… Zandular." She would bet there weren't many people by that name. It had to be the same man.

How…how did he find me? Not even Dumond could do that. A magician? What if… She stood up with a jolt. *Could he have placed a tagging device on my purse, my clothing?*

She raced to the chair where her purse hung. She turned it upside down on the table next to it and the contents spilled out. She felt the outside of the leather for any sort of device, then retrieved the lipsticks, papers, and brush that fell to the floor. She examined each item, but found nothing.

She let out a breath and went back to the bed. This time she pulled the covers over her and lay down. *"Bonne chance,"* Dumond would say "is better than being smart or good." She smiled at that one. Maybe that was all it was…dumb good fortune. At least, for now, he didn't know she was only a few meters from him. That was her kismet. Surprise was the best luck of all.

***

The alarm in his room went off at 6:30 a.m. Zandular figured he'd have enough time to eat breakfast, rent the Peugeot, and drive to meet this Monsieur Soreil. Last night's sleep interruption made him groggy, and he moved slower than he'd like. He imagined an older woman in the room a few meters from him…rich, probably, and spoiled. Most likely not French, but…American on holiday. The rich part intrigued him. She was definitely alone. He could show her a wonderful time…and make enough euros for his troubles… Nasser be damned. But first… He showered and dressed. He took his coat and then remembered. When dealing with men of weapons, one should be armed. He pocketed his gun and left. In the hallway were several people waiting for the elevator. The room over from his was where the ruckus occurred. He took note of the number. The receptionist could pay him in a different manner.

***

Soreil also woke early. Giselle was safely stowed in the basement along with jars of jam, vegetables, and bottles of wine. It took most of the afternoon to bury Karen. It was hard work to move dead weight any distance. But through ingenuity and his car he managed. Now, even he would have trouble finding her grave.

Dinner had been mostly a solo affair, although his captive was fed carefully. He attended to her bodily functions with the use of a rope tied around her neck. She behaved. This morning, though, she would be made to look presentable. Karen was nice enough to have plenty of clothes, if needed, for Giselle to choose from.

He cooked some eggs for himself, keeping an eye on the road that led to the house. He cleaned up, then went down the stairs to the basement. He found his prisoner curled in a corner tied head to toe.

"Bonjour," he said. "Sleep well?"

Her eyes widened.

"Well, it doesn't matter. I brought you some bread with jam."

She made no movement.

He fed her a few pieces at a time. "Now breakfast is done, I'm going to untie some of your bonds."

She perked up.

"Not free you entirely." He untied the rope that went from her ankles to her neck, but left the noose. Her arms were still tied behind her back. "There. Better? Stand up."

She didn't move.

"I'll ask you again, nicely."

She moved her legs slightly.

"That's it. Sit up."

He pulled the rope tight and ran his hand over her face and chin. "Your skin is soft and has such nice color." He ran a finger over her lips, then reached for her hair and sniffed. "Definitely could use a wash. Agree?"

Her breathing grew rapid. "Silly girl, I don't want to hurt you." His words had no effect. She tried to pull away, but the action tightened the noose.

She coughed.

"See what happens when you don't mind? You hurt yourself. Stand." He jerked the rope and she stumbled from her cot. He pulled and she followed, more like being dragged than walking to an open space in another part of the basement. Given the size, it must be where the owner washed down the vegetables or small animals. He tied the rope to a metal post. Then taped her mouth. When he finished, he warned her to only obey, otherwise… He gestured. He stepped away from her and went to another room. He stomped around and finally found what he was looking for. He hooked up the hose and returned.

He saw her tremble. "Don't be frighten. It's for your own good. I'm taking your clothes off. You'll feel better after."

Her face turned red, her screams muffled.

"There, there." He took a knife from his pocket and cut the straps of what was left of her dress. He then pulled downward and let it fall. Next, he ripped her bra, then her thong. The remains of what she wore pooled at her feet. He stopped what he was doing and gazed at his prize. It wasn't sexual but monetary. Her figure was apparent, despite the condition she was in. Her breasts were perfectly sized and firm, as well as her ass. He picked up the hose and thought of the euros. He turned on the spray. She immediately lifted her leg to shield herself from the water.

"It may be a little cold, but you'll get used to it." She hung her head in apparent defeat as he walked around her. The process took only a few minutes. "I'll get something to dry you off."

He disappeared into another room and found a horse blanket. He placed it around her and then led her back to the cot. He checked the time. There was about an hour to go. No need to dress her. Any buyer would want to see the merchandise as is. He left her in the blanket and went back upstairs to wait.

Chapter Thirty-Eight

Paris

J odie motioned for the waiter, a middle-aged man dressed in white shirt and black slacks.

"Was there something not to your approval?" he asked.

She gazed at the unoccupied chair in front of her as well as the empty glass. Her hand circled the rim. "It looks like my guest will not…"

"A different table, perhaps? One not so…eh…public?"

"*Merci,* that won't be necessary." She was about to ask for the check when she eyed her phone. "You know, I'll have another." She pointed at the glass.

The waiter hesitated, then, "Very well, *mademoiselle,* with a twist."

She nodded. As soon as he left, she called Hershel Joseph, who remained at the London embassy.

"Joseph, *shalom…*"

"Yehudite? What's going on? Isn't Zandular with you?

"If he was, I wouldn't have called. Listen, please, take down this number." She heard street noise in the background. "Where are you?"

"You wouldn't believe me, if I told you." She turned in her seat and looked out the picture window. "Did you follow me?"

"Yehudite, you ask too many questions."

"You might as well come in. Zandular isn't coming."

Her phone was still to her ear when the maître d' arrived with Joseph.

"*Excusez-moi, madame,* this gentleman says he was invited to join you."

She smiled, nodded, and put the phone down. *"Merci,* better late than never."

"Oui." The maître d' was about to turn when the waiter arrived with the drink. "Here you are, Madame. Would the gentleman care for…"

"Whatever she's having," Joseph said.

"Very well." The maître d' glanced at the waiter and they both left.

Jodie didn't wait for Joseph's drink. She took a healthy sip, then put her glass down. "So, why are you here?"

His face tightened. "We've lost too many today. The Ambassador suggested…"

"Ach. I can take care of myself."

"Of course." A smile flew across his lips. "Yehudite, we can't afford to lose any more. Enough. We don't know if this Zandular is a killer, arms dealer, or just in the wrong place at the wrong time. We do know that is not his name."

The waiter returned and set the drink down in front of him.

They both glanced at him. "Give us a few minutes," Yehudite said.

"I'll come back for your order," he said.

As soon as the waiter left, she told Joseph of Zandular 's excuses for not coming. Then she slid her phone to him. "You're a whiz at technology. That's Zandular's phone number. What are the possibilities?"

***

Inspector Ricard didn't sleep much. He woke almost every hour. He eyed the glow of the clock on the night table and urged it to move faster. Then he dozed, never drifting into a deep, rich sleep. It was about five when he decided the best thing was to get up, shower, shave, and have a little breakfast. It took only forty minutes to accomplish all those tasks. He turned on the small TV in the kitchen. The news program emphasized the weather and early traffic reports. He heard nothing further of the missing policewoman— Giselle Arrote. Time warred with him. No matter what he did, it didn't go faster. At a little after six, he decided to head back to the Hotel Millesime. The travel would eat up at least forty-five minutes, if not an hour. He figured he should reach the place seven-ish, not necessarily too early to disturb Mademoiselle Cook. It was 7:10 when he drove up the driveway. Otto had been replaced by a woman. "Catherine" was displayed on the nametag.

"Bonjour, monsieur," she said, her voice much too cheery for the early hour. "Welcome to Hotel Millesime."

He flashed his badge, and some of the joy left her face. "I won't be too long."

She nodded and stood by his opened driver's side door.

He reached into his pocket and withdrew the photographs of Giselle and Susan.

"Did you work the morning shift yesterday?"

"Oui. I worked from six in the morning to two in the afternoon."

"Did you see these two women?" He pointed to Giselle. "She was here at about ten, ten-thirty. She had on a black dress and short coat. A couple in a bluish color vehicle picked her up."

She studied the photographs. "Are they related?"

"Not that I know of."

"Hmm, that one," pointing to Susan, "I think I saw her

leave. It could have been afternoon…late. I was already off-duty."

"What about her?" He drew her attention to Giselle.

She took the picture and held it up toward the sky. "Non," she said after a while, "we were very busy around that time. I must have been parking a car. I'm sorry."

"Me too. If you would put my vehicle to the side. *Merci.*" He walked the few feet to the entrance weighing whether it was too early to call. Perhaps it was, but a life hung in the balance, and that tipped the scale.

***

The sun stretched its morning light into the darkened room of the safe house. Joseph turned on a small light by the desk in the bedroom and began to read the encrypted message from The Office," headquarters of the Israeli Mossad.

Of course, they had argued whether to go to the hotel Jodie had arranged for the tryst with Zandular. Joseph pointed out that communication between them and The Office wouldn't be secure. His argument carried the day. It was nearly midnight when they arrived. The tragedy of the day, along with the food and drinks, exhausted them. There was only one bed in the small apartment. It didn't matter.

"Ma cara?" Jodie asked. She sat up, drawing the bedsheet to her shoulders, then with her hand shielded her eyes from the light. "What time is it?"

"Rega," Joseph said. After a moment, he continued. "The Office has sent information about your friend. They've homed in on his phone. He's on the move."

"What? Where?"

"He's driving out of Paris."

"Out of… *merde.* We have to follow."

"I suggest you put on some clothes."

She looked under the cover and realized she wore only a tee shirt. "My God? Did you…?"

"I should be that lucky. You slept like a baby."

"B'seder." She jumped out of bed and dressed. She ran to the bathroom while buttoning her shirt. At the sink she splashed water on her face, then grabbed a towel on the way out. "Let's go. We have to follow."

In less than five minutes they were out the door. "You drive," Jodie said, "I'll monitor the phone."

***

Zandular felt good getting behind the wheel of the car. Since working for "the movement," he did it so seldom. It was taxis, trains, or someone else driving. Despite the cold weather, the sun made all the difference.

Traffic wasn't bad as he followed GPS directions to the A13 highway. He reached for the croissant that rode as the passenger. The French knew how to make pastries. Arab versions were good, but this was beyond. He washed his bite down with coffee, and then placed the cup back in the holder. He looked out the window at the passing scenery. He decided he always liked driving and he should do it more often.

He didn't know much about this Soreil. Nasser provided only sketchy information that his target may have the resources to acquire weapons or knew persons who could provide such equipment. The possibility that this trip could be a waste of time crossed his mind. However, if it did go well, he would have accomplished his mission. Paris, then, would be his playground…not a bad bargain. He thought back to the night at the La Villa Madame. If he could only find Susan again, or someone like her…*très magnifique.* He closed his eyes for a second and imagined.

Chapter Thirty-Nine

Stateville

For a man in chains, Monte acted as if he was chairman of the board. "How am I going to get that bitch here?" His smile widened. "Technology, that's how."

"You're full of crap," Shep said. "You're wasting our time."

Billy Dee leaned a little closer. "My partner may be right. He really doesn't like to be played with. Neither do I."

"I'm not playing." Monte's smile disappeared. "Look, life here isn't a joyride. I need to get out. I know if we work this deal, I have to perform, otherwise I'm back in this miserable place. It's the last place on Earth I want to be." He jiggled the cuffs on his wrist. "I told you she murdered the woman found in that house. I saw it with my own eyes."

Billy Dee gave him a look. "You told us that already."

Monte swallowed and looked at Billy Dee, then Shep. He continued as if he didn't hear. "I was fucking her. She was very much alive when that bitch, Susan, or whatever she's calling herself, dived into the room and smashed the woman with a hammer."

Billy Dee turned to Shep. "The guy," pointing to Monte, "loves to tell the same story. We get it. You didn't get your rocks off because you were interrupted."

Monte shrugged, "Yeah, I didn't."

"You better have something more than that," Billy

Dee said, "Like why were you there? Why was that woman there?"

"And what about the two dead guys in the other part of the house?" Shep chimed in.

"I found them that way," Monte blurted.

Billy Dee sat back. "I know you stayed mum with the Feds as well as us. You went down on an attempted murder of police officers and a weapons charge. Pretty light, if you consider what the charges could have been. Now either you spill everything, and I mean everything, or we leave you here until your sentence is completed."

Monte's body language suggested that he had just been deposed. He bit his lip, then was about to say something but stopped. He eyed Shep, then Billy Dee. A minute or two passed in dead silence.

"Okay," his voice barely above a whisper. "I'm going to give you a name. He…eh… You have to understand weapon dealers don't exactly advertise. There's a guy who knows another guy and so on. Susan or whatever, turned out worked, associated, with a man… Dumond."

Billy Dee worked on keeping his emotions in check. He quickly eyed Shep, then tapped his pen on the table. "Spell it."

"What? It's French or some shit. D-u-m-o-n-d. Anyway, she came to Chicago to get weapons for Dumond. The seller was that Serbian fruit wholesaler who wound up dead. The bitch admitted she did him." He stopped and stared.

"You told us that. Go on," Billy Dee said.

Monte looked as if he'd stepped into a cold pool and took his time to adjust to the temperature before answering. "Dumond was a hustler." His eyes flashed around the room. "…guns, booze, dope, maybe women too, not sure. He always found others for the cash. A fellow, went by the name Soreil, along with his broad, came up with the scratch. Her name, I think, was Karen. Dumond was the middleman. His customer was the SLA."

"Serbian Liberation Army," Shep interjected.

"Yeah. Right." Monte cleared his throat. "Anyway, Susan was going to buy the arms from that Serbian fruit dealer, Hugo, and ship it to Europe. The deal got fucked. Dumond disappeared, Susan escaped, and …eh…Soreil and his woman are in Paris now, searching for Dumond and their money." He leaned back, pulling the cuffs toward him. His gaze swept the room again, and without waiting for a question, said, "How do I know? I know. The SLA have people everywhere."

Billy Dee had taken notes. He lifted the pen near his lips. "This Dumond? Is he alive?"

Monte looked straight at Billy Dee. "You ain't see'n the forest from the trees, man." He wiped his mouth with his sleeve. "As your partner said, the SLA knows things, and I know things. As I said, I… I..," he took a deep breath, "know how to contact that bitch, Susan."

"There's enough holes in your story to drive a truck through," Billy Dee said, "but I'm gett'n the idea. You'll only give us Susan and in return you receive one get out of jail card."

Monte's eyes gleamed. "Now you talk'n."

✳✳✳

Paris

Susan was awakened by her phone. It emitted the first few measures of *La Marseillaise* informing her of an incoming message. Wasn't it only minutes since she'd closed her eyes? The time on her cell read otherwise. It was nearly ten a.m. She sat up. The room was bathed in shades of gray as edges of sunlight crept in. Objects could be distinguished. She cast an eye on the door. The chain remained across it. She listened for any hallway noise while holding the phone in her hand. Satisfied she was safe for the present, she looked at the screen and punched the message app. A video unfolded. An older man dressed in a long almost formal coat strolled in a garden using a walking stick. The following words scrawled across the bottom: retrouvez-moi aux Jardins des Tuileries l'après midi à 4 heures.

"Meet me at the Tuileries Garden in the afternoon at four p.m.," she whispered to herself, then gasped and covered her mouth. The figure looked like Dumond. They would often meet there. She was transfixed. *Could it be? Dumond alive?* She used her two fingers to enlarge the frame, but it made the details fuzzier. Her heart beat faster as she was locked into the fading image. *"Non,* come back." She pressed the message again. Only the words reappeared. *Is someone playing a joke? A gift from Zandular?* She found herself shaking. It was too much. She hurried to the bathroom and caught herself in the mirror. Worry lines parked themselves across her forehead, and her hands felt colder than ice. She turned on the shower and allowed the hot steam to wash over her. She had to think this through. Her life depended on it.

***

Chicago

Billy Dee sat in front of the TV. It had been a long day spent at Stateville and then on the way back listening to Shep discuss the matter with the higher-ups. By the time Billy Dee got home, it was after dark. A partial deal had been worked out with Monte and the State. Now he just wanted to relax.

He had one remote in his hand and picked up another. He pushed the On button on the white one and waited. Nothing. He tried the black one…partial success. The screen lit. He still didn't get how his new system worked. He went back to the white and hit the number 3 and then 2. *Nope.* He tried different combinations and succeeded only in viewing diagonal lines.

Janine must have been watching. She took the two clickers from him. She hit something on one and then the other. "Here's your basketball game."

"How did you do that?" He didn't wait for an answer. "What a picture. Lordy, LeBron looks like he com'n through the TV and hand'n me a pass."

Janine gave him that far-off stare. "He threw you the ball like I'm go'n to Paris."

"Don't start. We've been through that."

"The phone's ring'n," Janine said.

"What? I don't hear anything."

"That's because you deaf and have the stereo blasting… for a basketball game." She shook her head. "Are you going to get it?"

"You heard it. It's probably for you anyway."

"Uh-huh." She left the room. Seconds later, she shouted for him to get the phone.

He didn't want to tear himself away from the game. *Who be bother'n me now.* "Who the hell is it?"

"Come over here and find out."

He slowly got up and went to the kitchen and took the receiver from his wife. "Yeah?" he said.

"It's on."

"Who is… Monte?" Billy Dee asked.

"I told you I'd get to the bitch."

Chapter Forty

Versailles

Soreil kept watch from the kitchen window. It wouldn't be long now. He checked the time again. If this Zandular was anything like Dumond, weapons weren't the only commodity he was buying or selling.

In little less than an hour, he'd have money in his pocket. Giselle's naked image flashed before him. If Zandular was like most men, ach, the bitch will be his. He hoped the new owner made good use of her attributes. It pained him a little that her beauty would fade prematurely from what awaited her. *C'est la vie. Cows are bred for slaughter, no matter how pretty.*

He refilled his cup with coffee and sat at the kitchen table. As he sipped, it occurred to him there was still time…an hour or so…to test the merchandise, so to speak. She would be easier to sell if he knew from experience. He looked out the window at the soundless road. How could anyone live here for any long period of time? He was a city boy. A place like this was nice for a day or two, but the quiet got on his nerves. He licked his lips and glanced at the door that led to the basement. *A quick romp, what would be the harm?* His hand caressed the coffee cup as he thought of the softness of her skin, and visualized her round and luscious breasts. He started to get up. If Karen were here, she'd probably agree. Probably she'd have a go at her too.

Karen. He sat down. They were good together. She could smell a mark faster than he. She was emotional, no, passionate.

They'd had a good run, but like most things, there was an end. If it had been the other way around, and she'd had the gun, she'd be drinking coffee and he'd be buried. That was the consequence of their lives. In this situation, even she would resort to selling the bitch. Despite her passion, she was also practical.

He stood, checked the time once more, and glanced at the road. *Hell, how do you sell a car without taking it for a spin?* His heart beat faster as he headed toward the basement door. He rationalized. It was a way to extol the bitch's virtues.

***

Paris

Mademoiselle Cook sounded wide awake when Inspector Ricard called early that morning. She invited him upstairs. He suggested the hotel's café, but she insisted their talk would be better in the privacy of her room. He didn't argue further.

There was little wait for the elevator that took him to her floor. The corridor's heavy carpet suppressed the sounds of his footsteps. Her door was ajar, but he knocked anyway.

"Come in, Inspector, please."

He found her seated on a brocade chair next to an ornate table. A woman, he guessed, in her late forties. Age had accentuated her attractiveness. She wore a silk robe that barely concealed her breasts and the hem touched a little below her thigh. A towel covered her hair even though dark wet strands peeked out from under. He apologized for his interruption.

"I was already finished when you called."

"I'll get to the point without disturbing you further."

"You're not. Coffee? I can ring for it."

"No, thank you." He forced a smile and cleared his throat. "Otto the doorman…"

She bent forward and her robe slid up. "Excuse me, I do need a coffee and croissant. Otherwise, I can't think." She reached for the phone on the table. "I can order two just as easy as one."

Ricard peeked at his watch, and nodded. "Black, if you please, and a butter croissant. *Merci.*"

She smiled and ordered in a clipped tone.

"You must do that often," Ricard said.

"It's the way of the independent woman. If hesitation is detected you are done. *N'est-ce pas?*"

"I suppose."

She waved her hand as if to close the subject. "You were saying, Inspector, I spoke with Otto." Her hand subtly pulled the hem of the robe toward her bare thighs.

He caught her movement and cleared his throat again. "Yes, Otto told me you may have seen this woman, yesterday morning." He pulled Giselle's photograph from his pocket. He was about to show it when there was a knock at the door.

She held up her hand. "Breakfast." She stood and went to answer the door. The waiter brought in the order. "You can set it on the table, *merci.*" The uniformed man did as told. After he placed the serving platter, he poured coffee into two cups.

"Will that be all?" he asked.

"*Oui,*" she said.

He stood by the table and let a few seconds go by. "*Merci,*" he finally said.

Ricard sensed the man was waiting for a tip and it was obvious that mademoiselle in her petite robe was without money. He paid and the man left.

Madam Cook walked by him to close the door, then passed him again surely knowing she was giving him a bit of a show. She sat and reached for the coffee. "Where were we?"

Ricard had no illusions as to what was taking place. A part of him was flattered she considered him for a fling. Was it because he was an Inspector, or was it him? It didn't really matter. It wasn't the time or place, although...his thought went to Giselle, and unexpectedly sighed.

"Something wrong?"

"*Non, non,* not at all." He showed the photo. "Tell me what you saw yesterday morning."

***

Versailles

Soreil clumped down the stairs. He took a knife with him, just in case. He dared not use it, though, and damage the product.

She was curled as best she could with the blanket over her. He realized he'd forgotten to blindfold her.

"Just came to check on you," he said. "This will be over soon."

She stared.

He removed the blanket and gazed at her figure. It had been a while since he and Karen had had sex. Maybe if they'd had more of it... No matter. He undid the rope that led from her ankles to the noose around her neck but held on to the unencumbered end. Her hands were still tied behind her back.

"You are a beauty. You know." He ran his hand down to the small of her back. Despite the conditions her skin was luxurious. He then used his finger and tried to get between her legs.

The rope he held moved as she looked back at him. "If that's what you want, it would be best for us both if you untied my feet."

He was surprised she spoke, as well as her willingness to join. He put his hand on the side of her face and pushed down. "Quiet." He held the rope in one hand and examined her body again. *How could he give up such an opportunity?* The bulge in his pants made his decision easier. "If you do not obey, I will cut you to pieces," he said as he removed the knife from his pocket. "Nod if you understand."

She did.

"Bon." He slashed through the rope that tied her ankles. "Feels better, *oui?"*

He watched her move her feet a bit, probably to get feeling. He undid his pants and loosely held the rope that was attached to her neck. His focus was on her and what he was about to enjoy. He leaned over her shoulders and licked her skin. *How slender,* he thought, taking inventory. His hand slid down to her ass and stroked her cheeks, all the while calculating the price. He pushed her legs aside and massaged her pussy. He could tell she was not participating, but he was fully aroused. He was getting a little impatient. "The wetter you get, the less painful and more joy—"

He was unprepared for the speed with which she flipped to her side. The rope slid from his hand and in almost the same moment he reeled and gasped for air. Instead of pleasure, he cried out from the white heat of pain emanating from his balls. His knife fell off the cot. She kicked him again, then again and again. He folded into a ball, unable to protect himself. His last thought before darkness overtook him was the sound of Karen's voice. She was next to him and whispered as the blows kept falling.

"What a silly man you are, Soreil. A fortune just slipped through your hands. All because you thought with your dick."

Chapter Forty-One

Paris

Mademoiselle Cook was forthcoming to the Inspector. She gave him a partial license plate number, WW 24, written on a crinkled piece of paper. She didn't remember the rest of it. She was sure, though, it was a blue Ford van. He should have been buoyed by this information, but he wasn't. His mind wandered while he waited for the elevator. Why did she wait nearly twelve hours before realizing what had happened? What else gnawed at him was her tone. There was something… He considered the speed and surprise of witnessing a kidnapping as a partial reason, but then why remember it at all?

He replayed the meeting with her. He characterized her as self-absorbed and very much into the physical. She said she had just returned from her morning jog. Her body certainly indicated someone in shape. He smiled at her willingness to have him sample that part. Certainly thought of herself as dominant. Seemed economically comfortable, but who knew how she earned a living. He learned from the hotel management she was not a tourist. She reserved the suite every month for two weeks. Business? Mistress? *The French. We are anything but transparent.* So, what made her remember a partial license number and finally report it?

He scratched his lip. *I am getting old.* He could hear his

wife scold him not to overthink, but that was him. *Age and cynicism, not a good combination.* He was aware it was an excuse to do nothing. At least he finally had a lead.

He reached the ground floor and walked out of the Hotel Millesime. He retrieved his car and called in the description of the van and license plate to Officer Letrec. Ricard didn't have the patience to deal with the bureaucratic Systeme d'Immatriculation des Vehicules. That was for a younger person. To his surprise, Letrec called ten minutes later.

"I didn't think I'd hear from you so soon," Ricard said.

"Lucky for me I know someone at the Department."

"Bon. Who's the owner and where?

"It's a temporary plate registered outside of Paris, but the letters on the plate indicate it's a car, not a van. The best my friend determined was Versailles or Saint-Germain-en-Laye. Blue Fords are not unique."

"A car? She said it was a van. *Merde.* How many in each place?"

"She didn't count them. A rough estimate? Hundreds, a few less in Versailles."

"Email the list. I'll go to Versailles and you to Saint-Germain-en-Laye," Ricard ordered.

***

Versailles

Zandular had plugged Soreil's directions into the car's GPS. It worked well as long as he was on the main highway. Once out in the country, though, he relied on the scribbles he wrote. "Exit such and such, turn right, then go seven kilometers until you come to a fork in the road. There's a red barn, can't miss it, make a left." Easy enough, but every barn passed was red. He checked the odometer.

He was well past seven kilometers depending on when he began to look. *"Merde,"* he said in French and repeated in English, then Arabic. He could rely on his native tongue to truly express his feelings. He glanced at the clock. The time was getting close to ten. He thought of calling, but then Soreil would think him a fool. He would jeopardize his bargaining position. *If I can't follow simple directions, what kind of negotiator could I be?* No, the thing to do was back up and pay attention to the mileage. It took another few minutes to find a spot to turn. Ten minutes and nine kilometers later he came to a stop. There, on his right, was a red barn. A small wooden sign about two meters high pointed the direction to La Ferme de Robert.

***

Giselle was exhausted. Her kidnapper no longer moaned but lay motionless. She stood over him…staring. For a moment or two, she wasn't cognizant of his bloody face and the purple color of his genitals. Or that there was no other sound except her gasps. She stepped away and went to the other part of the basement. The hose was still there. She found the valve and, unlike before, the cold water calmed her as it washed away the violence. Still dripping, she returned to her cot and grabbed the blanket. The bastard hadn't moved. It occurred to her she should check if he was alive. She kneeled on his left side, her back to his face. She lifted his hand and placed two fingers near his wrist. Then the world blurred. She felt herself grabbed around her neck and pulled backward. She fell on the hard floor, and he jumped on top. She bucked her hips and arms to throw him off but even injured, he overpowered her. He held her down, and she stared into a face of rage. He spit out his words.

"I will have my way, you bitch. Today is your end."

He slapped her hard across the face. She screamed and he landed another blow.

"Shut up!"

She tried to get at him, but he slammed her arms and pinned her shoulders with his knees.

"You will not win," he hissed. "Better to stop your struggle. It will be less painful for all."

She cried and tried to move her head to escape another blow. Too late. She closed her eyes to lessen the pain. She felt him move. A second or so later, squinting, she saw him grab the knife that had fallen. Her thrashing ceased at the coldness of the blade against her throat.

"Bitch," his voice was steady, "I own you. Do you understand? You, whoever you were, no longer exists. Your life is no longer yours. You have no past and your future is what I grant."

The point of the knife indented her skin. "You are my slave to do what I want…own you, sell you, fuck you. Do you understand?" He grabbed her jaw. "Tell me with your eyes."

***

"Where is he now?" Joseph asked.

"*Rega,*" Jodie held up her hand. "I… what is going on?"

"Give me the phone."

"You're driving. I'll figure it out."

"How much ahead is he?"

"*Sheket!* I can't focus with you talking." She stared at the screen. The blinking dot that represented Zandular's car vanished. "It's gone."

"What?" He grabbed the cell.

"Careful," she warned. "I don't want to die on a French highway."

"Ach. He glanced at the screen, then the road, and after a few seconds, said, "Take it."

"So, what does this mean?"

"Use my mobile and call The Office. My guess is Zandular got off the highway and is in the countryside."

Her lips formed a question.

"GPS works well in the city, but still has trouble in the boonies. Understand?"

She heard but chose not to answer. Instead, she typed a code and pressed Send.

Chapter Forty-Two

Chicago

Out of habit, Billy Dee checked his watch. If it was 3 a.m. in Chicago, it must be 10 a.m. Paris time. Susan would have six more hours to decide if she was going to show. Of course, that depended on if Monte had succeeded in sending that video and whether she saw it. Protocol dictated he should let Inspector Ricard know. It was a simple decision. But what if Monte made it up? Yeah, Monte explained the idea of the video, but Billy Dee's knowledge of technology was limited. He had to trust the bastard, which led to even more questions. Even Shep voiced concerns.

"You still think'n about that phone call from last night at this hour? It ain't go'n to be daylight for hours." Janine asked, entering the kitchen. "By the look of you I already know."

"What?"

"You haven't even drunk your coffee. Now I know your mind all crazy. What the harm in tell'n the Inspector? Worse thing, it don't pan out. Maybe the girl didn't believe what she saw, or it frightened her. The Inspector can't blame you for what's in her mind."

Billy Dee looked up from the table. "You right about that." He drummed his fingers on the table. "Just don't want to be stupid. Our stoolie ain't the most trustworthy. Don't know if I even believe what I heard and if I don't, why should she?"

Janine put her hands on her hips and gave him a long stare. "Billy Dee, you ain't nobody's fool. You do'n the best you can with the four-one-one you got. If she goes to that garden, and the police not there…" Her voice trailed off.

Hearing Janine put it that way made all the sense in the world. There's as many reasons why Susan would show as she wouldn't. It was a chance. Let the Paris police decide how they'll play it.

He grabbed his coffee. "Damn, it's cold."

Janine took the cup from him and threw the liquid into the sink. "I'll make you a fresh batch. Go call."

***

Paris

Susan dried herself off from the shower while observing her reflection in the mirror. She imagined Dumond behind her, touching her wet skin with light kisses. He knew her. He knew every inch of her body and her mind. He knew when to be velvety and when to be a beast. It was a constant chess match, but not a game. It kept both of them alert and alive, and in their way secured a bond of trust. Was it love? Dumond thought that a dangerous word. Not that it wasn't there, but because it was an emotion, and emotions clouded the playing field. In the world they inhabited, that sentiment could lead to checkmate. At this moment, though, she wished. She closed her eyes and allowed herself to feel his lips, his hands as he undid her towel. She felt him brush against her, as she touched her breasts. A sigh escaped her mouth. Dumond seemed as real as he was in the video. She squeezed her eyes tighter and braced herself on the sink counter. Her hand brushed against something. She heard a crash and blinked, then eyed the fallen makeup container. The moment gone.

***

Inspector Ricard got on the A13 highway to Versailles. Traffic moved. Unlike most mornings where he could devour an entire baguette and only move several meters. He figured that whenever he got that list of blue Fords, most could be disregarded. It always came down to a few that fit. Anyway, he hoped. More like he prayed that Giselle was alive and he would be the one to rescue her. His imagination was interrupted by the ring of his phone. Letrec again? He punched the Receive button.

"Inspector Ricard? This is Billy Dee from Chicago." He paused.

"*Oui,* from Chicago, the detective," Ricard answered, not expecting the call.

"I hope I'm not disturbing you."

"*Non,* I'm driving. What can I do for you?"

"You know that picture I sent of that girl…Susan Dumond?"

"*Oui,* Susan."

"I think she may show up at that Garden the Tou…Touee…"

"Jardin des Tuileries. It is one of Paris's most beautiful attraction. You must see it one day."

"I'm sure, but did you hear what I just said. Susan may be at that garden at four p.m. Are you interested?"

Ricard took his eyes off the road for a second, then had to swerve back into his lane.

"*Oui,* what? This is, how you say, out-of-the-blue." He gripped the steering wheel a bit tighter.

"It is, isn't it. But, my source may have gotten a message to her. She expects to meet this dude, Dumond, at that garden at four p.m."

"Dumond! He is dead. Murdered."

Ricard heard Billy Dee swallow. "Oh. What you say, murdered? Who did it?"

"Sorry to admit, his death is still under investigation."

There was another long pause. "Look, I'm…I mean, we, Detective Sheppard and I, are… we made a deal with Jack Monte. He claimed he can find this Susan. I figure, you'd want to know. If she shows and you catch her, we've slapped each other's back. If not, Monte stays in prison."

"I'll do what I can. A police officer was kidnapped. She worked with me, and I'm determined to find her…. God willing…. alive. That is what interfered with our plans to bring you to Paris. I'll pass on your tip. *Merci*, Detective Jackson, I hope for the both of us."

"Me too. Lord have mercy."

Chapter Forty-Three

Versailles

Giselle's eyes told Soreil she had no fight left. He had won this battle but wasn't sure of the war. His knife was still at her throat, and time was running short. He didn't intend to kill her, at least not yet. Nor was he able to fuck her, given the beating he'd received.

He sensed it must be close to ten. Zandular would be arriving soon. Just thinking about that encounter made him nervous. The man would ask too many questions. Besides, the package he had for sale was not presentable. Zandular wouldn't want a woman whose face was black and blue. As Karen pointed out on many occasions, timing was everything, and right now was not the time.

He stared at his prize for a moment. He had not damaged her too much. Her face will heal and—thank God—he hadn't scarred her body. He squeezed her tit, and she yelped. He let out a laugh that turned into a gasp. What he needed was ice and a lot of it, but that would come later. He put his hand around Giselle's neck. "You are going to get up and we'll move toward the cot. I will cut you if you do something cute."

He got off her but kept his hand at her throat. He tried not to wince as he walked the few steps. "Now lie down on your stomach," he told her.

He placed his knee on her back and grabbed the ropes that were next to her. He tied her arms behind her back and used another for a noose around her neck. He pulled her by the leash and told her to get up. He led her upstairs to the kitchen. It was close to ten, but there was no sign of a Peugeot. He knew, though, he had to hurry. He found a dish towel and masking tape in a drawer. He used the towel to cover her eyes and then wrapped tape over the cloth and around her head. Then he did her mouth. "You are looking more helpless every minute. *C'est bon.*" He tied the end of the rope to the kitchen table. All the while, he kept an eye on the window and the road as he reached into the freezer for ice. *This will hurt,* he told himself as he put the ice in a napkin and applied it to his balls. "Jesus!" he yelled. "You will pay."

He went downstairs for his pants and slowly put them on. It was a painful climb back. He got more ice and as he was putting it into a cup, he heard the faint sound of an engine. He checked the window, and saw a dot. It was moving.

"We leave," he said more to himself than to Giselle. He untied his prisoner from the table and led her naked through the rear door. "You will not freeze."

He opened the car door and shoved her to the floor between the front and back seats. Once he secured her, he found a coat-like sweater that Karen left and threw it over her. He slammed the door shut and as best he could, maneuvered himself behind the wheel. He turned the car on and made a three-point turn toward the road. He accelerated down the gravel path, leaving a white plume. He saw the oncoming Peugeot but did not get out of the way. There was a screech of brakes and a hand gesture. He didn't stop.

***

Zandular made the turn toward La Ferme de Robert. The road twisted and curved as it continued upward. The rolling hills made a spectacular view. In the distance, he could make out a house. That must be Soreil's place. The road narrowed. As the house came into focus, he saw a dust cloud and the roar of an oncoming vehicle. It was coming right at him. He slammed on the brakes and pulled to the left. The approaching car narrowly missed him. "Idiot!" he yelled, and stopped to gather himself. After the pounding in his chest settled, he drove the short distance to the house and parked. There were no other vehicles around. He looked back toward the road, but didn't see anything. He went up the few stairs to the front door and knocked. When no one answered, he tried the door and it opened.

"Bonjour? Anyone here? He stepped into the small hallway. "Monsieur Soreil?"

He followed the corridor into the kitchen. There were spots of blood on the floor. He looked around, and pulled his gun. "Anyone?" he called. On the table was a cup full of ice; next to it was a pistol. He took the weapon and placed it under his coat. From the kitchen he noticed the rear and basement doors were open. He called Soreil's name and peered out the back way. There were tire marks on the grass. To say this was strange was an understatement.

He moved away from the back and looked intently at the stairs leading to the basement. If mischief were to occur it would be there. However, the lights were on. He crouched as he headed down, moving his gun hand from left to right.

He reached the bottom. There was a small room off to the right. A cot was against the wall. Ropes were on the floor, along with spots of what appeared to be blood. He stooped and touched one. It was fresh. *What the hell happened?* He straightened and walked the area of the basement. Other than a torn black dress, he found nothing else. He went back upstairs and stood by the kitchen window. What to do? Calling Soreil was the obvious. But nothing in the house made sense—blood on the floor, doors left opened, ropes, and torn clothing. Something definitely happened that made or forced Soreil to leave. Was it Soreil or… whoever ran him off the road. He gazed at the kitchen area again, then he heard a distant sound. He looked out the window. It was definitely a car and it was heading toward the house.

***

"Has The Office responded?" Joseph asked.

Jodie turned slightly while keeping an eye on the screen. "What do you think?"

He stared at the road. Seconds later, he darted over two lanes of traffic and exited the highway.

"Are you crazy? Why? You're going to kill us."

"We'll pull off and wait until we get an answer. If I keep driving, it could take us kilometers out of the way."

"Or we fall so far behind, we never catch him."

"It's the chance we take."

"Ooooh." She went back to her phone. "Come on, answer."

Joseph pulled to the side of a two-lane road. He shut off the engine. "We wait."

"I hate this," she said.

He glanced at her. "What do you hate?"

"Waiting. It seems that's all we do. We wait for someone to bomb us, or shoot us. We wait to die. We just wait."

Joseph smiled. "Yehudite, the rabbis tell us, life is the period between birth and death, but the *kuntz,* the trick, is what you make of it."

"Since when did you become a Talmudic scholar?"

"You don't see my *payes* and beard…an old Jew transformed

into a sabra?" He touched his ears. "Sometimes to wait is more important than to act. It allows for thinking."

She glanced out the window for a moment. "What great thoughts have you come up with?"

A beep from Jodie's phone stopped Joseph. "The Office found him," she said. "There's more."

⁂

The sign on the A13 indicated Versailles 2 kilometers ahead. Inspector Ricard moved over a lane to exit while on the phone with Letrec. He relayed his conversation with the Chicago detective, Jackson, and told Letrec not to spend much time in Saint-Germain-en-Laye. Instead, he needed to be at the Jardin des Tuileries before four.

"Choose two or three others and do not wear police uniforms," Ricard said, "There's a picture of Susan on my desk. Make sure your team has it. She's wanted in the States for murder and possible arms smuggling in Paris. Be careful."

Ricard left the highway and turned on a two-lane road toward Versailles. He went over the highway he just left and spotted a blue Ford getting on the A13 toward Paris. In the seconds it took, he caught a glimpse of the license plate....W. *Could it be?* His heart raced as he made a U-turn. The motorists he interrupted blared their horns, and one or two gave him the universal gesture. The race was on to find that damn car. His vehicle was equipped with a siren, but had no other police insignia. Surprise was on his side.

He accelerated well beyond the speed limit, weaving from lane-to-lane. He drove like a madman, surely scaring the hell out of the other drivers. He was aware that this display could also attract highway police, but he had no choice. Old as he thought he was, his driving ability hadn't diminished.

The skills he'd learned at the police academy all those years ago stuck with him.

Kilometer after kilometer flew by, but no blue Ford. Maybe he didn't see what he thought he saw. He reduced his speed to slightly above the limit and glanced at the vehicles in the other lanes. A sign posted on the right of him warned of a toll booth ahead. *"Merde."* Traffic slowed. He drummed his fingers on the steering wheel and followed the cars ahead. He kept searching… five cars to his right…. a dark-color Ford. He nearly leaped out of his seat. That must be the one. He edged closer nearly striking the vehicle in front. He stretched himself over the wheel. There on the license plate he read the letters, WW.

Chapter Forty-Four

Paris

Susan's hand shook as she picked up the fallen makeup container. The incidents since she'd returned to Paris were piling up. Paris was supposed to be her come-back… life after Dumond. She thought it possible. After all, he had introduced her to many of his contacts. Instead of success, she made mistake after mistake.

She scolded herself for letting the video get to her. Dumond also had enemies…lots of them. She knew that, but wasn't careful. Any one of them could have sent it. Then she thought of Karen and Soreil. They were a real possibility. More likely them than Zandular. They definitely had it out for her. She'd wound up at this hotel partially because of them. The thought settled her. Once you figure who, strategy becomes easier. Her hand stopped shaking. She preened for the mirror and smiled at the image. Her beauty still intact, and ready to be used as a weapon.

She took a brush to her hair. As for Zandular… He had his own problems. His name was identified as the bomber in London. He may be dead there, but, damn, he was very much alive and staying down the hall. Coincidence? "Hmm…" She shook out her hair. What a predicament. Zandular in the hotel, but he didn't know where she was. While Karen and Soreil still hunted for her. Were they all together? She held a fistful of her hair. *Non,* probably not. The one thing in common, though, was Dumond and her connection to him. Meeting at the Jardin would solve that for either one. She let her hair fall and placed her hands on the counter. She leaned toward the mirror and studied her face. What if…

***

Versailles

Zandular watched from the kitchen window as the car came into view. Was that Soreil or someone else? It didn't make a difference, given the evidence of the struggle he'd found in the house. He checked his weapons to make sure both were loaded, then searched for a place. The kitchen? He'd be target practice sitting at the table. The front closet, but then he couldn't see. He heard voices outside…female and another male. He was too far away to decipher the language, but it didn't sound French. *"Alqarf! Merde!* Whoever they were, were coming closer. He had to get out…the basement. He took the stairs so fast, he almost fell. When he regained his balance, he went inside the room with the cot. The stairs cut his line of vision so that the person would be almost upon him before he saw the target. Hopefully it would work the same for his opponent. He put his ear on the doorpost. Except for his breathing, there was no other sound.

***

"There's a Peugeot parked in front," Jodie said, "you think it's Zandular's?"

"There's nothing else around. It must be him," Joseph

said. He stopped their vehicle several meters away from the parked one. He leaned over and examined her phone. "That dot says it's him."

"Why here? Jodie asked, glancing at the house and the foliage around it.

He shrugged. "Why did Eve eat the apple? Riddles. He drove here for a purpose. He must be waiting for someone—an arms deal in the making. Too bad we're going to spoil the party."

Jodie nodded and pulled her weapon from under the seat. She held the Uzi and loaded it. "Not the bang he thought he was going to get."

Joseph did the same with his. "You mean he had the chance to die in your arms?" He gave her a long look.

"Don't get any ideas, Joseph. His would have been for duty to country. If that's what it took to discover his disfigurement on his ass… nothing more. Besides, I'm not allergic to penicillin."

"At least he'd have the chance."

"Poor boy. Concentrate on the job."

They got out of the car as quietly as they could. Jodie stooped low to the ground and came up to the Peugeot. Joseph went around to the back of the house. She slowly rose and peered into the driver's window, her weapon aimed. She glanced inside and saw no one. She tried the door. It opened. Inside were a pair of sunglasses and directions, along with a name scribbled on a torn sheet of paper. She rummaged through the glove box and found a rental agreement in Michael Zandular's name. She placed the contract in her pocket. The suspect confirmed. She waited by the car until Joseph returned.

"The back door looked open," he said, "and there were fresh tire marks on the grass."

She thought for a moment. "This is Zandular's car. I have

the rental agreement for it." She patted her pocket. "We didn't see a vehicle going past us, and the Peugeot's hood is warm. That indicates he's here." She viewed the house and grounds. "Somewhere here."

Joseph pointed in the direction of the house.

Jodie nodded and followed. Joseph was correct about the back door. They entered the house and noticed droplets of blood on the kitchen floor and a cup of melted ice on the table. She stepped toward the hallway leading to the front, but Joseph pointed to the open basement door. They looked down the stairs and saw the area lit.

"We'll get killed going down those stairs," Joseph whispered.

Jodie contemplated the odds. "Yeah, certainly a possibility." She stepped away and moved toward the kitchen table, motioning Joseph to follow. "I have three ideas. We take the stairs and hope for the best. I call out to him and try to persuade him to surrender, or..." She eyed the kitchen area then swallowed. "We burn him out."

"Set fire to the house?"

She nodded.

"That could be a diplomatic disaster."

She shrugged. "Maybe, but according to The Office, Michael Zandular, aka Ahmed Zayid, showed no mercy in Tiberias. According to our specialists, Zayid poisoned Shoshana by transmitting penicillin during sex. Clever but horrible. He's a killer. Besides, he's going by the same name as the bomber of our Embassy. How much compassion does he deserve?" She didn't wait for Joseph to answer.

"Michael," she called from the top of the stairs. "I know you're down there. We could have had a hell of a time the other night." She waited a few seconds. "Yeah, it would have been great. I've researched you. Your bedroom techniques are something every woman desires. Come on out, Michael."

No response.

"Listen, Michael." She switched to Arabic. "I know who you are. Your secret is out. If you stay down there, you will die. I assure you." She listened for a sound. Not hearing any, she resumed. "I am offering you your life. You understand? You get this one chance. If you don't take it, the wrath of your God and mine will fall on you."

She stepped away from the landing and whispered to Joseph, "Light the match."

Chapter Forty-Five

Paris

Soreil congratulated himself on escaping Versailles. He sailed on the A13 with no one the wiser. Karen will never be found. The only other witness to her death was the girl who was tied and bound. Other than a few grunts, she'd been no trouble.

The drive made him remember another friend who had a garage in the 10th arrondissement, near the Gare du Nord. A crime-ridden area that tourists and decent people avoided. Andre thrived. There wasn't a criminal venture he wasn't into. He would see the girl and know immediately this was a business opportunity. He kicked himself for not thinking of Andre earlier, although Karen would never had consented. She despised everything about him. He was the lowest of the low, according to her, and she would shower after any meeting. Andre was a rogue, but a necessary one. He made the call.

Soreil was proud of himself. This time, the girl would be sold to a buyer who did not need much persuasion.

He caught the sign for the toll and slowed his speed. He turned slightly and observed the girl, who remained obscured while lying on the back floor with a long sweater covering her. With any luck, the toll taker wouldn't see. He kept a hand on the steering wheel and with the other tapped his pockets. *"Merde,* my gun." He glanced at the passenger seat. *How could I be that stupid and leave it at the house?* He let out a breath and returned his eyes to the road. The vehicles in front edged forward. He was the fifth in line. While waiting, he glanced out his sideview mirror and spotted a car in the lane over. It nearly struck the one in front. What an idiot, he thought and moved ahead. He rolled up to the booth and put the window down just far enough to pay. His foot hovered over the accelerator. The toll taker didn't move from his seat and waved him by. *"Au revoir,"* Soreil said under his breath; the gods were still with him.

* * *

Ricard saw the Ford go through the toll. It took another three minutes for him. He calculated the car was at least three kilometers ahead, given time and distance. He gazed at his speedometer and figured in his head the speed needed to catch up. He turned on his flashing lights but kept the siren off as he weaved through traffic. He assumed the Ford was going into Paris. If that was wrong, Giselle's life would be lost.

Traffic was medium, as he made up the distance. His mind, though, multi-functioned. Even as he kept an eye out for the Ford, his conversation with Detective Jackson popped into his head. How was this Susan mixed into all of this? No demands had been made regarding Giselle. As far as the police were concerned, she was officially "missing." Was it accurate to believe Giselle was the target of the kidnapping? What would they want from her? The photos of Susan and Giselle flashed before him. He concluded they had a similar look. Then it occurred to him. Dumond. He was the link. Whoever was in the Ford thought they had Susan. They set up this meet at the Jardin des Tuileries after realizing their mistake. All of this confirmed what he thought happened in the first place.

He chuckled at how his brain concocted this neat package. Life had taught him, though, nothing was ever that simple. It was a theory, some of it probably true. At least it reaffirmed his belief that Paris was the destination. It was worth informing Letrec of such a possibility.

***

Paris

Susan, dressed as an old woman, sat on one of the benches at the Jardin des Tuileries. She had gotten there around three-thirty p.m. She made herself into the generation that held a copy of *La Monde* in her gloved hands instead of an iPhone or iPad, and appeared to read the paper. As the hour grew close to four, she changed locations to another bench where she and Dumond would meet. She peered from the page and observed a tall blondish fellow along with a woman walk slowly on the path. They seemed to take in the garden, but their movements betrayed that appearance. They would glance around, then look at their phones, especially when a woman was in the vicinity. They did it to her.

"Excusez-moi," the blond man began, "My girlfriend and I couldn't help noticing you. We told my cousin from America to meet us. We think she's lost. Have you been here long?"

Susan put her paper down. She wore thick glasses and a cloth coat with a scarf wrapped around her neck. A duffel bag was scrunched beside her. She made her voice scratchy when she replied. "I am taking my afternoon rest."

"It's a bit chilly, don't you think?"

She nodded and smiled. "It builds strength and every

minute I steal to be among this beauty is a moment well spent. *N'est-ce pas?"*

The man nodded and glanced at his girlfriend. He showed the woman his phone. "This is a photo of her. Her name is Susan. Have you seen her?"

Susan studied the picture. It was an image of her taken in Chicago. *"Non,* I haven't." She brought the phone closer to her glasses. "Pretty girl. She must take after you," and after another glance gave the cell back to him. "This is a beautiful place to be lost."

"Merci," he said and held the phone in his hand. The girlfriend said something Susan didn't hear. The man nodded. "Thank you again," and they moved off.

Susan waited several minutes before she left her bench. She knew those two were flics and inept at undercover, thank God for that. What they unknowingly disclosed was it wasn't Zandular or Soreil who set this 4:00 p.m. meet. *Non,* not them. She started to walk. If it wasn't them… Ah, the photo. How did the flics have it? Only one person had the knowledge and opportunity…Monte. The son-of-a-bitch wanted revenge and sold out to the cops. She shouldn't had ignored her first inclination.

She walked out of the Garden onto the Place de la Concorde. Monte had to be dealt with once and for all. Le Sanseveria café was up the street. She went in and found a seat near the back where she could observe. After ordering a coffee and croissant, she took her iPad from the duffel bag and plugged in Monte's name along with SLA and Chicago. Voilà, his story appeared along with the names of the detectives. She then went on the Illinois Department of Correction website and learned the crimes Monte was serving time for. Murder wasn't one of them.

***

Giselle felt each bump of the road. She knew time was her current friend, but it wouldn't last. She had to free herself. During the drive, she had bitten through the tape over her mouth. While the bastard was singing along with the radio blasting, she rubbed her head against the rear door frame and eventually was rewarded. She was able to see a little. Then she worked her arms. Her sweat dampened the ropes, and by twisting and turning them, the bonds loosened.

"You will earn me many euros," Soreil said in between one of the songs. "My balls are also doing better, and before you leave me I will take my pleasure. That's a promise, my little whore." He resumed his singing.

Under the sweater, she deftly moved her hands to her neck and undid the noose.

"I want to be fair with you," he called out, "we are going to the Gare du Nord section. I'm sure you are familiar with it. You, once being a flic and all. We have an appointment. You'll be shown to all the best people." He laughed. "What a life you'll have. After they are done with you, I imagine you'll be shipped to Marseille and from there…well, who knows. Your tits may not be as round or your ass as firm. A pity."

She felt the car turn, then slow. *He must be off the highway and entering Paris.* Depending on traffic and the time of day, she had fifteen to twenty minutes. A lifetime on one hand, or a minute.

The car stopped. Her heart raged against her rib cage. Stoplight? Was this the end? The radio was still on, please… Then movement again. She blessed her God.

"Merde," he said, a short distance later and shut the music. "I've come this far. Just what I needed." His voice came closer. "You better not move."

She did as she was told. She realized they were motionless. He heard him lower the window. Words were exchanged.

She felt a blast of cold air, a shout, then a door slammed, and the car took off.

"Goddamn flics," he yelled.

Police. This was her chance. The speed in which she got up surprised her as well as him. She grabbed him around his neck in a choke hold.

"What are you…get killed."

The car crashed. She let go of him and leaped, naked out her door and opened his. She dragged him out. Her fury landed punch after punch, easily overcoming his defensive moves. He crumpled to the street, but she continued to pummel him.

"Giselle, Giselle, stop. I have him."

"You're under arrest!" she screamed while landing blow after blow, until she heard her name through the din of her own voice. She stopped and looked. She couldn't believe it. "Inspector… Inspector…oh my God." She sank to her knees, hugging his pant leg and sobbed.

Chapter Forty-Six

Chicago

"It's two in the morning," Janine said, "are you make'n a habit of waking in the middle of the night? Why you look'n at your phone?"

Billy Dee ignored her and got out of bed. "Unbelievable," he said, "I'm go'n downstairs."

"You what? Go to sleep."

"Can't." He put on a robe and trudged down the stairs to the kitchen. He pulled a chair from under the table and sat. Hunched over, he stared at the email, then read it again. He shook his head out of disbelief and wondered if Shep got the same message. He punched in Shep's number. His finger hovered over the green button when he remembered he could text. If Shep was up than they'd talk. He sent Shep a message, then looked around the kitchen. He might as well take advantage of not sleeping. He opened the refrigerator and grabbed bread, sliced ham, a package of cheese…

"And what the hell do you think you're doing at this hour?" Janine asked.

Billy Dee closed the fridge and maneuvered the goodies onto the table. "Didn't hear you come down. Make'n a sandwich."

"You know that ain't good for you."

He took two pieces of bread and was about to unwrap

the deli paper that held the ham. "What's wrong with this? It got protein, some carbs, and veggies." He glanced at the fridge. "You stopped me before I got the tomato and lettuce along with the good mayo."

"You never go'n to learn. You just don't eat—" A chirp from his phone interrupted her lecture.

"Hold on," he said and picked up his cell. "Janine, I got to talk to Shep. He just messaged me. Go to bed. I'll be up later."

"At least eat only half, for God's sake."

He waited until Janine left, then called.

***

Versailles

"You sure you want to do this?" Ricard asked, holding his phone. It was early morning and he was about to have his eggs and toast with his just-brewed coffee.

"*Oui*. I'm sure. I can't thank you enough, but…I must go back. That pig, Soreil, murdered the woman he was with and buried her near the house. I think I have an idea where."

"I can pick you up…say in forty-five minutes."

"*Bon, merci, merci.*"

Ricard hung up. He swished the omelet around on the plate without taking a forkful. Not even twenty-four hours had passed since he'd found Giselle. He had stopped the Ford on a street off the A13 in Paris. In his excitement, he made the rookie mistake of being in front of the driver's door instead of behind. The son of a bitch knocked him down with it and drove off. If it hadn't been for Giselle, Soreil would have gotten away. She was rushed to the hospital. After filling out reports at the station, he drove to the same hospital for his cuts and bruises. He was discharged in the early evening but waited. It was close to midnight when Giselle was allowed to leave. He drove her home. On the way she repeated what she'd told the arresting officers.

She tried not to be emotional, but the tears came anyway. She clung to the ill-fitting clothes someone gave her. He was concerned enough to ask if she wanted him to stay with her.

"You've done more than enough," she said, her voice soft. "I'm a big girl and have to learn to get over this."

He walked her into her apartment. "If you need or change your mind, call."

She nodded and closed her door. She probably slept little, which was why she phoned so early.

He threw the eggs away and gulped his coffee. A few minutes, later he was out the door.

As he pulled up to Giselle's building, she stepped outside. *"Bonjour,"* she said.

"Bonjour, how are you?" He didn't need her to answer. Her face told him everything. "Have you had anything to eat? Coffee?"

She played with her hands. "I showered and felt better, but I don't have an appetite."

He drove a few blocks and stopped at a café. "You have to have something. I'll get you a croissant. You take coffee with cream? *Oui?"*

She nodded.

He came back to the car a few minutes later. "Just the smell of the pastry and coffee will make you hungry."

She smiled for the first time. "You are so kind, Inspector…"

"It's Alain."

She gripped the bag of food, her dark eyes on his face. "Alain."

***

There wasn't much conversation. Her memory as to directions was remarkable. They didn't get lost even when they came to the fork in the road. For some reason, she knew of the red barn and definitely remembered the small sign, La Ferme de Robert. She pointed to the narrow road.

"This leads to the house," she said.

He gave her a glance. He saw her face pale as she gripped her hands. "It's okay, Giselle, the bad guy isn't here."

She wiped her eyes. "I know, but…" She took a deep breath. "I know…"

The road climbed and twisted, he observed the house in the distance. Coming closer, there were cars and fire engines parked on the grass. A Versailles policeman stopped them several meters from the house.

Ricard rolled down his window. "What the hell happened?" He showed his identification. "This is Officer Giselle Arrote. She was the kidnapped victim."

"Kidnapped? When?" the officer asked.

"Paris hasn't sent reports?"

The officer scratched his head. "*Non,* nothing. We're here because of the fire to the house. There's some damage, but it's contained. Seemed like something happened in the kitchen and basement. The owner is over there." He pointed to a youngish man dressed in a long shearling coat.

Ricard opened his door. "Stay here," he said to Giselle. "Let me find the inspector on this case."

The officer pointed to the other man next to the owner. "He's the man you want."

Ricard began to walk. He had taken several steps when he heard someone behind him. "Giselle?"

"I can't sit in the car."

The two men stood near a parked Peugeot. After introductions Ricard asked the owner if he knew someone named Alex Soreil.

"*Oui.* He's an acquaintance, but I haven't seen him or Karen in a while. Why?"

Ricard explained what had happened.

The owner turned to Giselle. "I am so sorry. I didn't know Soreil in this way. I am shocked. He and Karen were like a happy married couple."

"They don't speak well for marriage or for humanity," Giselle said, "Soreil shot Karen and buried her. I think I know where." She pointed in the general direction of the surrounding fields. She lowered her arm and stared at the Peugeot. "This wasn't here when Soreil brought me."

The Versailles inspector spoke up. "We checked it out. It was rented out of Paris to someone named Michael Zandular. The idiot left the rental agreement in the front seat. If he's anywhere near, we'll find him."

***

Tel Aviv

"So?" Joseph asked.

Yehudite rolled over on her side. "You want a rating?"

"No, silly, I am full of energy and smiling from ear to ear."

"*Tov maode.* You are very good. I am content and enjoying this luxury. The bed, the sheets"—she turned toward him—"and you."

He pulled her close to him. "We did it."

She laughed. "Yes, we did. Wait. What are you talking about?"

"Zandular. What are you talking about?"

She blinked. "The same. It didn't take long after we threw the homemade Molotov cocktails into the basement. I didn't know vegetable oil had other purposes. Zandular would have been slow roasted if he hadn't run up those stairs."

"He was shocked when he saw me."

"I wouldn't say that." She rubbed her arm. "Okay, he knocked me down and you took the fight out of him."

"Zandular was out for hours. A good thing, too. It took a while to get to De Gaulle airport."

"Only because you drove like a priest."

"Nonsense. I kept with traffic. Besides, it gave you time to work your magic with the Embassy and find us a plane," Joseph said.

"I do have magic, don't I?"

He kissed her. "Yes, you do."

"You know, as we lie in this beautiful hotel room, Zandular's crew will be rounded up. It is a beautiful day for us."

He kissed her shoulder. "Yes, a beautiful day, but it will never stop. Today we're on top. Tomorrow…"

She put her finger to his mouth. "Don't spoil it. We must celebrate again."

"For country?"

"No, for us."

Chapter Forty-Seven

Chicago

"Did I wake you?" Billy Dee asked.

"Nah, I'm usually up at this time in the morning. What time is it? Two-thirty?" Shep asked.

"You answered the text."

"Yeah, well, I got the same email, and I would have called you, but you beat me to it."

"What do you think?"

"I think Monte is slimier than we thought."

Billy Dee picked at the remaining crumbs of his sandwich. "Yeah, he's a bad dude. You think the email was from Susan?"

"Probably."

"Lord have mercy. How she found all that information and then us. Jesus, she's very good…better than the Paris police."

"Hold on there, Billy Dee. She kept company with people like Monte and Dumond. She had a head start."

Billy Dee opened the fridge, pulled the ham and cheese out, and made another sandwich. He bit into it.

"You eating at this hour?"

"All this stuff made me hungry," trying to disguise his chewing. "Besides, the old lady is sleeping. Look," he swallowed, "whoever wrote this, and it probably be Susan, supplied a lot of detail as to who killed Dumond and Monte's role. I'd think the French would like to know."

"I agree."

"I'll get hold of Inspector Ricard. You, deal with the muck-ety-mucks and the prosecutors. I have a feeling Mr. Monte better brush up on his French."

"Yeah, okay. What about Susan? She's no angel, and she's still over there."

"True, but here's the thing. Monte's little scam to get her didn't work. He's useless to us. Why pay for his upkeep when the French have a better chance to make homicide stick? As for our Susan, I'm sure the French will help us after they have this information. Eventually she'll turn up, there or here."

"Enjoy your sandwich. I'll start work on the higher-ups."

***

Paris

"Billy Dee, I can't believe it. Paris. I forgive you," Janine said.

"Forgive me, for what?"

"Everything you ever done. My heart stopped when you told me Inspector what-ever-his-name—"

"Ricard. Alain Ricard."

"—invited us to Paris, and it's spring. I can't believe it."

"You will when I show you all the bills from your shopping."

"Hush. Now where did the inspector say he'd meet us?"

Billy Dee took a crinkled paper from his pocket. "Café Les D-o-e M-a-g-o-t-s. Strange name for a café calling itself magots."

"Billy Dee, you don't say the 'o-t-s'. It's pronounced 'oh'.

"Yeah, since when you speak French?"

"Practice. Anyway, am I dressed okay?"

In Chicago, he would have absently nodded or said yes.

But staying in this ornate room at the Millesime Hotel, he took his time studying his wife of so many years.

"You'll knock them out," he said.

She smiled and glanced one more time at the mirror. "Should we call a cab?"

"I think the place is around the corner or something. Besides, it's Paris and it's spring. Let's walk."

The Inspector met them at the entrance of the café and led them to a table.

"I am so pleased to finally meet you and your wife," he said, and kissed Janine's hand.

"Oh my." Janine held on to the back of her chair.

"This is my wife," Inspector Ricard said, pointing to Giselle who was already seated. "We married a month ago."

"Congratulations," Billy Dee's eyes locked on the new bride. Janine tugged his sleeve as they all sat. "We have a lot to celebrate." Billy Dee turned to Ricard.

"*Oui,* we do." He raised his hand and a waitress approached.

"*Bonne apres-midi,*" she said. "My name is Danielle and I will be your server."

Ricard nodded. "Champagne for the table. Laurent-Perrier La Cuvee Grand Siecle?" He looked at Billy Dee.

"Sounds good to me."

"*Bon.* I'll be back with the glasses and Champagne."

***

Danielle, after several minutes, served her guests. She caught wisps of the conversations between the women... marriage, husbands, life. She expertly opened the bottle and poured. The men toasted to the success of Monte's extradition to France and the closing of the Dumond matter. Later, she brought food to the table, then after-dinner drinks. Over coffee, the men discussed Susan and wondered as to her whereabouts. The Inspector claimed she'd disappeared into thin air.

She didn't let them see her smile.

She had changed her name, cut her hair, and made it blonde. Dumond had taught her well on how to disappear. She worked on weekends at this café. This was the place Dumond had brought her when they first met. She surveyed the room. At the very table where the Inspector and his guests sat, Hemingway ordered bottles of Lafite Rothchild. Over in the next corner was Picasso and his many female admirers. But the one who held court who was most admired as well as hated was Rene Hardy. A hero of France to some and a traitor to others. Such was France and such was life. Her life was good for now.